Destroy

DEADLY HEARTS, BOOK 2

EVE NEWTON

Destroy
Deadly Hearts, Book 2

By Eve Newton

Copyright © Eve Newton, 2022

Without limiting the rights under copyright reserved above, no part of this publication may be reproduced, stored in or introduced into a retrieval system, or transmitted, in any form, or by any means (electronic, mechanical, photocopying, recording, or otherwise), without the prior written permission of the copyright owner.

This is a work of fiction. Names, characters, places, and incidents either are the product of the author's imagination or are used fictitiously, and any resemblance to actual persons, living or
dead, business establishments, events, or locales is entirely coincidental.

Preface

Dear Reader,

Please note that this book contains heavy triggers of rape, self harm, familial child abuse (not shown) and mental distress.

For reference the scene of rape is in Chapter 1. This is not an overly graphic scene, the details are sparse but you are aware of what is going on.

Please note, though, that this book is dark and includes scenes of BDSM, with power play, blood play, knife play and DD/LG.

This book also includes scenes of M/M.

Please be aware that everyone deals with trauma in their own way, and the way Ruby attempts to get over hers is true to her character as I, the author, have written her.

Happy Reading!

Love Eve x

Chapter One

Ruby

I can't help but let out a groan of pain.

Cold steel is pressed to my throat. My own fucking switch blade. That angers me more than this whole situation combined. How dare he use my own weapon against me. Fucking asshole.

"Quiet," he hisses at me.

"Fuck you," I hiss back, and pay for my comeback.

His face comes really close to mine, and with a twisted smile, he drags the blade across my throat. Not hard enough to do any real damage, but enough to make me bleed. He knows his stuff. That will leave a scar...if I get out of here alive. I'm starting to think that isn't going to happen. My arms and legs feel like lead weights.

I close my eyes and stifle the whimper of defeat that threatens to come up. I've lived through worse.

I've lived through worse.

"Finished," D.I. Smith says, proudly.

I force my eyes open when he slaps the outside of my thigh.

Staggered is the word that comes to mind. I'm absolutely staggered that he is showing me his art of me trussed up, mostly naked and stabbed in the gut.

My keen eyes notice he is quite talented, but c'mon. He doesn't honestly expect me to praise him, does he?

Apparently, Boomer thinks I should because he buries the tip of the blade into the side of my neck.

"Very nice," I mutter.

"Such a beautiful subject," D.I. Smith says, and almost lovingly places the sketch pad on the stool before he turns back to me.

I do not like the look in his eyes.

"Don't worry," Boomer whispers in my ear. "You won't even feel it."

"Feel what?" I murmur in dread and then feel a jab in my upper arm again. I moan when my head goes woozy, my vision blurry and my hearing goes foggy. My leaden limbs get even heavier, until I stop feeling everything. I don't even feel the stab wound in my stomach anymore. It's a welcome relief, but only for a split second because Boomer's words come back to me.

What is D.I. Smith going to do to me that Boomer wants to *numb* me?

Boomer moves away from me, and I feel my legs moving. I think they've untied my ankles, but I can't tell. I can't lift my head to look.

I let out a surprised squeak when I'm dragged half-way down the table so that my ass is on the end. I only know this because I can see D.I. Smith looking over me now, from in between my open legs.

"No," I mumble, shaking my head as the fear that hits me is familiar and real. "No!"

I want to struggle, but I can't. I am completely immobile. "Boomer, please," I beg him, knowing it will be futile.

I can only watch as Smith pulls his cock out of his pants. There is silence in the room apart from my desperate sobbing to Boomer as he then produces a small foil packet. He rips it open and then unrolls a condom onto his erect cock.

"No," I slur, my lips not moving as they should. I don't even think my voice box is working properly now. "No, please, no."

I can't go through this again. I can't. I can't come back from this. I hope that Boomer does kill me now because this is it. The end.

I squeeze my eyes shut, screaming in my head for this to stop. I am motionless, voiceless.

A nobody.

A nothing, except a breathing sex doll.

I feel the motion of him thrusting, but that is all. From far away I hear a soft grunt, followed by a few sharp pants and then a louder grunt.

I don't want to open my eyes when I hear a zipper. I don't want to know what's coming next. I just want to fade into the oblivion that Boomer has injected into me and die there.

I send out a silent apology to my men for giving up and not trying to fight harder, but then there is nothing.

Unfortunately, my eyes open sometime later. I groan with disappointment, hating the fact that I wished for death and didn't get it. Who knows what more I have to endure at the hands of this psycho? I'm all about the psycho, don't get me wrong, but this guy has seriously lost the plot. I move my head and then realize that the rest of my body is mobile too. I lift my head, the eerie silence of this cold, dark room settling around me. I'm back in position in the middle of the table, my ankles retied, the knife still stuck in my gut.

I choke back a cough and flinch when it sends rockets of pain shooting through me. Yeah, whatever Boomer gave me has worn off. He has wadded a cloth up around the knife to staunch the bleeding. I have no idea how much blood I've lost, but I can smell it. I can smell my sweat and fear and the stench of this place all around me.

But one thing is very clear to me.

I'm alone.

Boomer isn't here.

Frantically, I start to work my right hand, trying to loosen the rope around it. A small ray of hope lights up in front of me and I do my best to ignore it. I try to convince myself that this is too good to be true.

But still, I wiggle and turn my wrist, trying to get free. The rope burns me, cutting into my skin, but I don't let it stop me.

Eventually, with a soft cry of pain, I squeeze my hand free from the rope. I freeze, expecting Boomer to come out of the shadows and tell me how I'm never leaving here, but there is nothing.

I swallow, the sweat forming on my upper lip from the effort I've put in to release my right arm. But it *is* free. I now have my other wrist and two ankles to get free.

Quickly.

There is only one way that is going to happen, and it makes all the blood rush straight to my head when I think about it. With grim determination, I grip the handle of the knife sticking out of me. Biting down on my bottom lip, hard enough to draw blood, I pull it out of my stomach with a loud gasp. The blood bubbles up and gushes out of the wound. I can't let it stop me. I have to ignore it and carry on. I move the bloodied cloth over the wound and reach up with the knife in my loose grip to slice the rope free from my left wrist. It takes longer than I'd hoped. I'm as weak as a kitten and about to drop the knife.

I tighten my hold on it and once the rope is cut loose, I force myself to sit up with a low growl of agony. I press the cloth to the hole in my gut with my right hand, while my left works at the rope around my ankles. Boomer really didn't do his research on me. He should've removed the knife if nothing else. He clearly didn't bank on me pulling it out of myself to get free.

The seconds tick by.

Left ankle free.

Swap hands.

Set to work on the right.

Soon, with sweat dripping down my forehead and into my eyes, my hair stuck to my head and every cell in my body screaming with pain, I slide off the table and stumble in the direction of where I know the door is.

I'm no fool.

I know it's going to be locked from the outside, but I'm armed and fucking dangerous. My brain is just about functioning enough to formulate a plan of action. I press my back against the wall on the opening side of the door. I inhale deeply and check the wound. The cloth is soaked in my blood, but I can't let it get to me. I have to ignore it. I grip the knife in my right hand and wait.

How long?

Who knows?

Time has lost all meaning in this room.

My knees wobble and my head swims, but still I stand there, trying not think about what happened to me.

Suddenly, I hear the locks being opened on the other side of the door, making my heart thump.

"You've got this, Rubes," I murmur to myself, tightening my hold on the knife as much as I can. My fingers feel like overcooked spaghetti, but there is no way I've made it this far to fail. I may have wanted to die on that table, but I'm not on the table anymore. I'm on my feet with a few centimeters of steel between me and freedom.

The door opens, making me squint from the light pouring in.

I take a breath and then stick my foot out so that Boomer trips over it when he crosses the threshold.

"Fuck," he mutters, stumbling and dropping the bag of groceries he was carrying.

With a battle cry of sheer rage, I lunge at him, knife raised and stab him in the back as hard as I can.

"Argh!" he cries out and bucks as I pull the knife back out again. I have just about enough strength left in me to do it again. I have to make it count.

He turns towards me, and I duck low, screaming as the agony shoots through me from the stab wound. But I'm low enough to jab the knife straight into his cock area, making him scream like a girl. Hell, my scream was deeper than his, the fucking pussy.

"Jesus Christ," he wails and drops to his knees.

My hand is still around the hilt, and we stare at each other for a second, maybe two before the fear and rage, the humiliation and torment rises, helped along by a massive dose of adrenaline.

I pull the knife out and shove him back, straddling him as I stab him in the chest, crying tears of fury and anguish.

I draw the knife out and stab him again.

And again.

My tears mingle with his blood. My blood seeps out of me and drops on him, but I barely notice it.

I just keep pulling the knife out and stabbing him.

His cries fade and he goes quiet.

I know in my head he is dead, but I can't stop. I can't let

go of the blade. He tortured me. He stood by and watched as I was raped. He *helped* my rapist. He is just as bad as Smith, and I will make him pay.

Eventually, I run out of everything. I leave the knife embedded in the side of his neck and roll off him, panting and scrunching my face up against the pain that has come flying back.

"Get up, Rubes. Get the fuck up," I mutter and roll over, getting to my knees and then my feet.

I stumble to the door, falling twice before I make it to the threshold. I grab the door jamb to steady myself and then I cross over into the light. Falling straight into the strong arms that grip me tightly with a loud, "Fuck!"

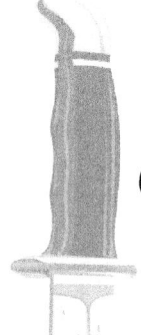

Chapter Two

Declan

Ruby falls into my arms with a loud curse and my heart stops beating. Just for a second. It's not enough to see her to bring me back. I'm too lost. I grip her arms tightly.

"Declan," she sobs, and then her knees buckle.

Ramsey is there for her. Catching her as she falls. "Ruby," he murmurs and lifts her into his arms, cradling her. "Fuck, she's hurt badly."

I close my eyes and breathe in deeply before opening them again. "Get her home," I bark out and then step over the threshold.

It's dark, and dank, and the stench of blood is everywhere. I walk forward, not even checking to make sure that the men behind me are leaving. I stop when I see the body of a man stabbed more times than I can count. There is blood everywhere. He has a knife sticking out of his neck, which I bend down to pull out. There is a small gush, but that's it. This man has been brutally murdered and bled out within minutes. He is as dead as they get.

"Ruby," I murmur and then I feel it.

The darkness lifts slightly, but only in the sense of my soul returning to ache for the woman I love. "What did you do to her?" I mutter and turn, striding quickly back to the door.

They've gone. Bundled her into the waiting car and took her away from here, home and safe.

I didn't even check to see if she was okay.

Turning back around, I enter the room further, taking in the instruments of torture and the table with which she was clearly strapped to.

"Jesus."

There is blood all over it. She is badly hurt, and I didn't even look at her. But the other men have her. She is safe and I am here to learn what the fuck happened, so she doesn't have to talk about it just yet.

If she survives.

I glance around and spot a bag on the floor next to a stool. I go to it and lift it up, rooting through it, looking for something, anything that will fill me in on this crime scene. It appears to be sketching materials.

I shudder when I think that this Boomer fuck undressed her and tied her up to draw her.

The sound of a scuffed shoe on the concrete makes me stash the knife in the bag and then turn around. "You," I say, narrowing my eyes and striding over. "You're that policeman that Ruby pays off. How did you know she was here?"

The Detective Inspector gives me a wary look before he clears his throat. "I was tipped off," he says and looks around. He flinches when he sees the dead body, but then his eyes go straight to the bag that I was searching through.

My blood runs cold.

I lunge forward and grab him by the collar, shoving him

up against the wall. "You already knew she was here," I growl. "Didn't you? Were you part of this? If you hurt her, I will fucking rip you to shreds."

He holds his hands up calmly. "I have no idea what you're talking about," he says.

"Like hell," I snarl and pull the handgun out of the back of my pants and shoot him in the left knee. The shot is muffled by the silencer, but his screams are loud in my ears.

I drag him by his collar over to the table and throw him on it. "Did you hurt her?" I ask.

"No," he says, shaking his head, frantically clutching at his knee. "I didn't, I swear. She was already here. Boomer took her. I like to draw, he said he had something that I'd like. I didn't know, I swear."

"Liar," I state and shoot out his other knee. "Try again."

His wail of agony goes on for longer this time, but I wait patiently. I am a very patient man. I have to be in my line of work. I cross my wrists in front of me and shush him until his cries turn to whimpers.

"I swear, I had nothing to do with this!" Smith rasps. "It was all Boomer."

Something is off. I can't quite place my finger on it, but this doesn't add up. "Why are you here now?" I ask.

"I left my bag," he mumbles, indicating the bag on the stool.

"That's yours?" I ask casually and cross over to it. "You like to draw? You like to draw half naked, tied up women?"

"I can't help the compulsion," he pants. "I didn't hurt her."

"You don't strike me as the sloppy type. Why did you leave it? So you could come back and draw her some more?"

"Yes," he mumbles.

"What did Boomer do to her?" I ask.

"He stabbed her and injected her with some stuff. I don't know what it is. He...he..."

I turn back to him. "He what?"

Smith licks his lips and looks to the left. "He raped her."

It feels like someone just reached into my chest and squeezed my heart in their hands. "How do you know that? Did you watch? Did you stand by and do nothing while he violated her? Did it get you off watching that?" I take two steps forward when he doesn't answer me and position the gun under his chin. "Answer my questions."

"I watched. He made me. I didn't want to stay," he stammers.

"You didn't try to help her?" The ice in my tone is clear even to my own ears.

Ruby. Oh, Ruby. I'm so sorry.

"I couldn't. You don't know that man. He was a fucking psycho," Smith cries.

"And you aren't?" I ask steadily. "What kind of man stands by while a helpless woman is assaulted?"

He drops his eyes.

Something still doesn't feel right.

"It was you, wasn't it?" I ask so quietly, I don't think he heard me at first. "You were the one who raped her."

"N-no," he chokes out. "I swear, it wasn't me."

I nod slowly. "See, I think it was you and there isn't a chance in hell you are walking out of here alive on the charge of watching, so you might as well confess your sins..." I dig the gun further into him. "Tell me...was it you who violated her?"

"No," he whispers. "It was Boomer!"

"Wrong answer," I murmur and pull the trigger.

His head snaps back, and he drops to the table, falling over the other side and landing in a dead heap, on the cold, bare floor.

I pick up the bag, shoving the gun into it and walk over to

the metal table with the torture instruments. I find what I'm looking for. No good torturer walks around without his blow torch, in my experience.

I grab it and test it. A flame shoots out and I nod to myself. Walking back to the body of the Detective Inspector, I bend down and fire up the torch. I hold the flame to the cheap material of his shirt, and it goes up like a Tiki after a few seconds.

I step back and pull the hip flask of whisky out of my jacket pocket. It's not for drinking. Never for taking a sip. But you never know when you need to set a fire to cover your tracks.

Striding over to Boomer, I look down at him, taking in a small sense of pride at Ruby's handiwork and then dump the contents of the flask onto the dead man. Then I light him up and drop the blow torch, walking out of that room as the fires burn hotter and quicker behind me. I close the door and head out onto the street from this dingy alleyway and walk towards the nearest bus stop.

It is time to go to Ruby and take care of her now.

She is going to need it after what she has endured. She is going to need extra care. It hurts my heart to think about how she must be feeling, but I push it aside. This isn't about me.

I board the bus and pay my fare, smiling at the old lady in the front seat. She smiles back, a big happy beam and moves aside to offer me the seat next to her.

I accept and sit next to her, the bag clutched tightly in my hand as we head back into the bustling city center from this rundown part of town. I will find my stashed vehicle for use in emergencies, so I can get to Ruby, tell her it's all over and help her move on from this trauma.

One step at a time.

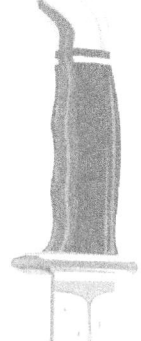

Chapter Three

David

Staring out of the window from Ruby's sitting room, I can barely breathe. She is in a bad way. Stabbed and bleeding heavily, practically naked and shivering. Probably in shock and God knows what else.

I had to call Michelle, the off-the-records doctor. Before Ruby passed out in the car on the way home, she explicitly said no hospitals. I get it from a business perspective but from a personal one, I'm terrified.

"She'll be fine," Layton mutters, coming to stand next to me.

"We don't know that," I mutter back.

"How is she?" Ramsey's voice rings out and we both turn to see Michelle walking into the sitting room from the hallway.

"Not good," Michelle says bluntly. "She needs to go to the hospital. She needs a blood transfusion amongst other things. I've patched her up as best I can but..."

"No hospitals," I croak out. "You know she can't."

Michelle sighs. "I get it, but..."

"What blood type is she?" Ramsey asks, interrupting her.

"A Positive," Michelle replies.

"I'm A Positive. Do the transfusion here," he states. "Can you?"

"I can," she says slowly, "but it will have to be live. I will have to feed your blood straight into her."

"Then do it," he growls and marches down the hallway to Ruby's room.

"I need the tubes from the car," she mutters.

I'm about to follow Ramsey when Michelle's progress out of the front door is halted by Declan.

He skirts around her and strides across to me. "How is she?" he asks quietly.

"Bad," I say. "Really bad. She's lost too much blood."

He closes his eyes for a second. "It gets worse," he says quietly.

"What do you mean?" I ask. "What did you find in that room?"

"Apart from a dead Boomer, a lot of stuff I wish I hadn't," he replies grimly.

"She killed him?" I ask.

"She more than killed him. I think he was dead long before she stopped stabbing him," he replies.

The tinge of pride and lust in his eyes is hard to ignore. I get that. Death is his business. For me, it's slightly more gross. I'm glad I wasn't the one who found him.

"What else did you find?" Layton asks as Michelle returns with another bag and goes straight to Ruby and Ramsey.

"Boomer wasn't the only one involved in this," he mutters. "D.I. Smith also played a part." The air of menace that drops over him sends a shiver down my spine.

"Smith?" I ask with a frown. "What does he have to do with it?"

"*Did*," Declan corrects me, making it clear the Detective Inspector is no longer with us. He inhales deeply and shakes his head. "He violated her."

I stumble backwards as if he has punched me in the gut and then ripped my heart out. "No," I say firmly. "No, that didn't happen."

"It did," he says. "Look, it's happened and now we have to go to Ruby and take care of her. We let her down by not being there to protect her and we have to make it up to her, if she will let us. I'm of half a mind that she will tell us all to fuck off, and to never darken her doorway again. And, to be honest, I wouldn't blame her. How did we let this happen?" he growls.

"She snuck out," I protest, but knowing it's feeble. Declan's right. We *should* have been paying more attention. We should've known she'd do something stupid that would get her in trouble. "Fuck," I mutter. "If she doesn't tell us to fuck off, we should anyway. We are useless to her."

Tears spring into my eyes and I turn away from the other two men. I feel a hand land on my shoulder and squeeze gently.

To my surprise, it's Layton who speaks. "All we can do now is make sure something like this never happens again."

"How will she even be able to look at us knowing how badly we let her down?" I ask quietly.

"We don't let her fall deeper into the pit of despair she must be in right now. This is the second time she has had to deal with this, she survived once, she will survive again," Declan states and then curses when Layton and I turn back to him, shock on our faces.

"Second time?" I ask, confused. "What do you mean? She's been abducted before?" I add with dread, but knowing in my heart that's not what he meant.

He just shakes his head and then walks slowly to the hallway, his brief pause screaming his emotions so loudly, there is no need for words.

"No," I say, shaking my head. "How can she come back from this?"

"She will," Layton says. "She's strong and she will. We will help her."

"We don't deserve for her to forgive us."

He sighs. "Look, David. I know you feel guilty, but that isn't helping her right now. We need to pull ourselves together, go in there and be everything for her because she is going to be a broken china doll that needs piecing back together, even if she says she isn't. She has been through too much, and her mental state is fragile as it is, if what Declan says is true. Can you do that? Can you be strong for her?"

"Yes, of course," I mumble, humbled by his words. But I'm not like him or Declan or Ramsey, even. I'm just a regular guy with no real strength to speak of, and emotions that bubble up uncontrollably. I can't just shove them down and ignore them. It's not who I am.

"Still be you," Layton says with a glimpse of that sexy smirk. "Just focus on healing her, but on things being normal. She won't want to be treated any differently."

I nod, wondering how he knows so much about Ruby when he only met her a few days ago.

I follow him down the hallway slowly, my heart slamming in my chest when I see her in bed, propped up against the white pillows, her dark hair tangled and bloody, her face puffy and pale. She is in the process of being hooked up to the blood transfusion thing, her eyes open but devoid of any spark.

Declan is staring at her, the longingness shown openly for her to see, if she was to look. But she doesn't.

Her stare is out of the window and doesn't move, not even when I sit on the bed next to her and take her hand.

"Hey, Rubes," I say.

She doesn't answer me. She doesn't even move.

It's only when Declan, whose hovering is starting to annoy Michelle, drops to his knees in front of Ruby that she moves.

But only to flinch and pull her hand out of mine.

"Back away from her," Michelle says. "She doesn't need you four crowding her."

Silently, we watch as Michelle finishes up and picks up her bag. "I have a phone call to make. I'll be back in a few minutes to check on her progress."

I follow her out and catch up with her in the sitting room. "When you said other things...what did you mean?" I ask.

"She needs a rape kit," Michelle states quietly. "Convince her to go. This arsehole will only get away with it if she doesn't do something."

I frown at her. "That's not fair," I start, but she shushes me.

"I know you care about her," she says. "Convince her to get the rape kit done. She will also need to be checked for STI's and pregnancy."

"Jesus," I mutter the bile rising in my throat.

"I'm sorry to be so blunt," she says, her voice softening slightly. "Talk to her." She turns and leaves me staring after her alone, and for the first time in a really long time, *lonely*.

Chapter Four

Ramsey

I rest my head on the cushion that I stuffed at the back of my head when I sat down to give Ruby my blood. I won't lie, it gives me the icks, watching it leave me and enter her, but I would give her every last drop if it meant saving her. The doctor asked me a bunch of questions that luckily, I could answer. I only gave blood last week, so I've been screened recently. She wasn't keen on letting me donate again, but I wasn't taking no for an answer.

"You feeling okay?" Declan asks me quietly.

"Yeah, fine," I say.

Ruby has closed her eyes. I don't know if she's asleep or pretending to be so we don't talk to her, but either way, it's too quiet in here.

David returns shortly after and sits on the bed again. Ruby lets out a small groan, but doesn't open her eyes.

Her breathing deepens signifying that she has gone to sleep now so I ask the question that has been hanging over my head since I scooped her up in that alley practically naked and bleeding.

"Does anyone know if she was...raped," I mouth the last word, just in case she hears me.

Declan nods grimly confirming my worst fear.

"Fuck," I mutter and close my eyes as my head spins. "Is he dead?" I ask, not opening my eyes yet. I can't. I can't look at her. Not out of *anything* to do with her, but because of the shit feeling that we let her down when she needed us.

"She killed Boomer. I killed the fucker who touched her," Declan whispers.

I lift my head and open my eyes in confusion. "There were two of them?"

"Long story for another time," Declan says, indicating Ruby with his head.

"Is he really dead?" I ask quietly.

"Yes," he says, sounding slightly insulted that I would question him.

"This is going to be difficult," I say, knowing this for a fact. A girl friend in high school was sexually assaulted. It took her years to get over. I still don't think she is. She cut off communication to all her friends a long time ago and dropped off the radar.

"Ruby is strong," Declan says. "With our help, she will recover from this."

"I hope you're right," I say, my gaze taking in Ruby's beautiful sleeping features. "He tried to slit her throat," I blurt out.

"No, he knew exactly what he was doing. That was for pleasure, not purpose," Declan replies, kneeling on the floor again next to her. He takes her hand gently and kisses it.

"I'm back, Princess, and I will move mountains to help you through this," he whispers.

I sigh and rest my head again.

My eyes start to close, but I'm jarred awake when Michelle bustles back in and declares that I've given enough blood for now.

I grimace when she removes the tube and then rub my hand over my face. My injured hand is aching, and my ribs are sore.

"I've got another visit. I'll be back as soon as I can," she says.

I nod and watch her go. "Someone had better ring the club. None of us are going to be in later."

"It's fine," David says. "I've closed it tonight. Rubes will just have to take the hit."

"Thanks," she mutters, surprising us.

"I knew you were faking," I joke lightly.

"How else would I find out what you wanted to say about me behind my back?" she mumbles, her eyes still closed.

I lean forward and run my hand lightly over her head. I kiss her forehead conscious of the need to pull back if she doesn't want me in her space. "Anyone ever tell you, you are a devious little Madam?" I ask.

She makes a noise that sounds like a laugh, but is hollow and harsh. "No, but I like it."

"Find that hard to believe," I murmur, taking my hands off her. She needs to know I'm here, but that I'll back off when she needs me to.

"What? That I like it?" she asks wearily, opening her eyes.

"That no one has ever told you," I correct her, and she smiles. A soft, almost normal smile before she sighs.

"Michelle leave any painkillers?"

"Yeah," I say and lean over to hand her two ibuprofen.

"That all?" she complains.

"It's all she had. She's coming back with some stronger stuff later," I tell her what Michelle told me earlier.

"Great," she grumbles but takes them from me anyway.

I hand her a glass of water. "Small sips."

"Thirsty," she mumbles.

"Small sips," I say, taking the glass from her.

"Asshole," she whines and closes her eyes again.

I smile and sit back. She is a fighter and I fall more in love with her than I could ever have imagined.

David takes her hand again and she lets him, but she is falling asleep again.

"Promise to make it up to you," David murmurs.

She smiles. "Yeah, you will," she says, and then grimaces as the pain gets too much for her.

"Sleep now, Princess. We will be here whenever you wake up," Declan murmurs.

"We will be here, always," I add. "We will never leave you again."

"You didn't leave me," she protests weakly. "I left."

"And when you are feeling all better, Daddy is going to smack your arse about that," Declan says with a soft smile.

She chuckles, but then her face falls. She sighs, her eyes opening again. "You know, don't you?"

"Yes, we know," I say, taking her hand again.

"It wasn't as bad as last time," she says.

Last time?

My eyes shoot to Declan's. He gives me an apologetic look. Seems everyone knew about it, except me.

"How so?" Declan asks, "if you want to tell us."

"Later," she says and then goes silent.

"Whenever you're ready," I say and clench my jaw to stop the ache in my heart. She has suffered so much, and we can do nothing to help her. What good are we to her?

"Let's all get some rest," I mutter and David leans over to switch the lamp off. He lies down next to her, but not touching her. Declan turns on the floor to lean against the bed. I stay in my chair and Layton crosses to the window to stare out of it silently until it goes fully dark. None of us move a muscle and eventually, I fall asleep.

Chapter Five

Layton

It's late. I prowl around the house for the umpteenth time, submerged in darkness. I'm not leaving anything to chance.

When Michelle arrives back around midnight, I let her in and silently follow her to Ruby's room.

Declan is awake, but still in the same position on the floor next to her. The other two men are asleep. Declan jumps up when he sees the doctor and moves out of the way.

"Ruby," she says quietly. "I'm going to have to give you an injection."

"No," she mumbles. "No injections."

I frown, curious why she won't take the morphine the doctor is offering her.

"Ruby,'" Michelle says.

"No. Injections," Ruby grits out. "Just give me tablets. I'm fine."

I see Michelle grimace and root around in her bag. She

takes out a small bottle of pills and hands two to Ruby with a glass of water. "Go back to sleep. I'll be back in the morning."

Ruby nods and settles back down.

Michelle indicates with her head that I should follow her out, which I was going to do anyway.

She pulls a small black zip up pouch out of her bag. "Morphine. Give it to her when you can talk sense into her."

I nod and take it. There has to be a reason why she doesn't want the injections, but I'll try anyway. She must be in a hell of a lot of pain.

I let the doctor out and lock up behind her.

Then I do another sweep of the house, making sure all the windows and doors are locked up tight.

Reassured that Ruby is safe for now, I head to the kitchen and root around for some hot chocolate, which I find stuffed in the back of the cupboard, a month out of date. I snicker, but put the kettle on to boil anyway.

As soon as I have my hot chocolate in a big steaming mug, I sit at the counter on one of the fancy leather stools and contemplate my next move. *Our* next move. I am satisfied that Linda is safe from harm, even though I see now it was my own paranoia that thought she was in danger. I am also satisfied that Boomer is dead. Declan hasn't said much about it, but I figure Ruby really went to town on him. It just proves once again how strong she is. Both mentally and physically. Not many would've been able to do what she did after losing so much blood. D.I. Smith, on the other hand, is something I need to know more about. Did he suffer? Was he screaming in pain when Declan killed him? I fucking hope so.

"Hey," Ramsey says, striding into the kitchen with a yawn. "Can't believe I've slept so long."

"You've had a rough couple of days," I point out.

"So have you," he replies. "Have you had *any* sleep?"

I shake my head. "I'm good. Need to know Ruby is okay before I can even think about that."

He nods. "Yeah."

"I didn't mean that you shouldn't rest, just that I can't."

"I get you," he says, not offended.

I watch as he silently opens the fridge and starts to pull a load of vegetables and chicken out. He reaches over for a kitchen knife out of the block and gets to work on chopping veg.

"What you making?" I ask.

"Soup," he says. "Ruby will need something nutritious when she gets hungry."

I nod. "You know what you're doing?" I ask with a smirk.

He laughs. "Been cooking for myself since I was thirteen. Pretty sure I know my way around the kitchen."

"Yeah," I say and then take the plunge, needing to say my piece after what Linda told me earlier. "I heard about your mum."

He freezes for a moment, but then continues chopping. "Oh? Linda tell you?"

"Yep. You know our mum knows everything and everyone back in the old neighborhood."

He nods slowly but keeps chopping. "Hmm."

"Are you going to see her?"

"Nope."

Chop. *Chop*. CHOP!

"Easy tiger. I'm just asking." I hold my hands up.

"She can die alone for all I care," he spits out. "I hope she fucking does. Cunt."

I raise an eyebrow, but don't say a word. I know the shit he went through with her. Alcohol and drugs, cheap prostitution to bring money in for more drugs and booze. Not a way for any child to grow up.

"No more said," I murmur.

"Thanks," he says and goes back to his soup making.

"Everything okay in here?" Declan asks, sauntering in all cool and whatnot. I see what Ruby likes about him. His job is just icing on the cake for her. She gets off on the thrill.

"Yep," I say and take a sip from my mug. "Listen. I need to know what you did to that arsehole," I growl.

"Did you make him suffer?" Ramsey asks, stabbing the knife into the chopping board as he fixes Declan with a fierce glare.

"Not nearly enough," he replies and heads for the coffee pot that someone remembered to put on earlier. Probably David.

"Details," I say.

"I shot out both of his kneecaps and then blew his head off before I set his dead body on fire. I also burned Boomer's body. That reminds me…" He disappears into the utility room and comes out with a brown leather bag.

"We need to get rid of this." He pulls out a bloody knife.

"Is that the one Ruby used?" I ask, standing up and taking it from him. I rinse it off in the sink and then throw it in the dishwasher.

Declan nods. "I also think it was the one that he used to stab her."

"Jesus," Ramsey says and pulls the knife out of the board to carry on chopping.

"I want to take her away from here," Declan states. "She already agreed to come to Ireland with me. I want to move that up. Leave as soon as Ruby is on her feet. She needs to get away from here."

"And us?" I ask.

"Of course you'll come," he says. "But you will have to find your own place to stay. My mam is staunch Irish Catholic. Mary Gannon will just about tolerate me bringing Ruby into her home and sleeping in the room next to her. You all arrive as well, and she'll be throwing holy water on us while she prays for our damned souls."

I chuckle. "I hear you. But that raises the question, will she accept Ruby? She doesn't need to be taken into a hostile environment."

"Mam is dying to meet her. If I know her, she has already booked the church for our upcoming nuptials, so you don't have to worry."

"I find it odd that you told your mum about her. Does she know what Ruby does? What *you* do?" Ramsey asks.

"Obviously not. Which part of Irish Catholic did you not get?" Declan asks.

"So what does she think you do?" I ask out of curiosity.

"Personal Security," Declan replies and I nod, accepting that completely.

"We need to plan out our next move," I say.

"Not without David," Ramsey says, bringing a pot of water to the boil before he throws the veg into it.

"Our very next move is to get Ruby up and showered," Declan says. "Layton, that's your department. You are capable of handling her both physically and emotionally. She knows your touch and she trusts you."

I can't help but feel pleased by this. Although I already knew I would be the one to take care of her, it's nice to know that I don't have to fight with the other men in order to do so.

"Ruby's awake," David says, coming quickly into the kitchen. "And determined to get on her feet.'

"On it," I say and move over to the doorway, following David back to Ruby's room, and hoping that she isn't going to reject my offer to help her.

Chapter Six

Ruby

As soon as I see the back of David, who has run off to bring in reinforcements, I use the nightstand and the bed to haul myself to my feet. I let out a soft cry, allowing myself the weakness because I am alone for the time being. I steady myself and take a small step towards the bathroom. And then another. Once I get going, I don't want to stop the momentum, so I keep going. I grip the door jamb and take a slow breath before I carry on. I reach the toilet and lift the lid. Ever so slowly, I lower myself down to the seat by gripping the toilet paper holder and the basin countertop.

"Aaah," I whisper and close my eyes as the pain from walking subsides slightly. Luckily, Michelle didn't waste time in slipping a pair of panties on me before she got to work on my wound. She found this loose, oversized Mets jersey in the drawer and dressed me in it after she patched me up with only a local anesthetic to numb the pain, which she jabbed me with before I could protest, and slapped a waterproof bandage on it. No way was she coming at me with an injection that was going to knock me out. Or any injection at all, if I'd had my say. I clench my jaw as the men come filing into the bathroom.

"Seriously?" I ask. "Can't I even have a pee by myself?"

"You shouldn't have tried to get here on your own," Layton says.

"What do you mean *tried*?" I snap. "I'm here, aren't I?"

Finally finished peeing, which was like a fucking racehorse, I grab some toilet paper. I wipe awkwardly and drop it into the toilet. Then I stand up, again using the holder and counter as leverage.

Layton tuts at me and leans over to flush it. Then he steps back. "Where do you want me to start?" he asks quietly.

I almost weep with relief that I don't have to ask for his help. "Teeth," I say, running my tongue over the fur.

"David, go and get a stool from the kitchen," he orders.

David runs off and returns shortly, placing it near the basin.

I slowly and painfully slide my ass on to it. Layton gets to work with my toothbrush and the toothpaste.

"Open up," he murmurs and presses the button on the electric toothbrush.

I do as I'm told, and he inserts the vibrating brush into my mouth. If this were *any* other time but now, I'd be laughing.

"Spit," he says, and holds my elbow as I lean over the basin.

This goes on for a full two minutes. Fuck's sake. What is he? A closet dentist?

When we are finally done with my teeth, he steps back again. The other three men are still hovering silently.

"What's next?" Layton asks.

I love him for leaving this all up to me and stepping back to give me space. I hate that he has to. I hate that I need him to.

"Hair," I whisper.

He turns on the shower. I freeze, but then he holds his hand out for me to grip and haul myself off the stool. He lets me go and grabs the stool, placing it in the shower. It will be ruined, but I give him a grateful glance. My fists clutch the hem of my shirt. I can't. I just can't.

"You don't need to take it off," Layton murmurs.

I nod before I step gingerly into the shower. Using the taps to steady myself as I slide back onto the stool, my back curves as I hunch my shoulders against the warm water. Layton removes his jacket and I gasp.

"Oh," David murmurs when everyone clearly sees what is etched into his arm. My name gouged into his flesh.

Layton ignores everyone's reaction and leans into the shower, scooping up my hair to drench under the pleasantly warm water. Not too hot, not too cold. Just right. I sigh and close my eyes as he works his fingers through my bloody, tangled hair, gently massaging the shampoo into my scalp and rinsing it out. I'm disappointed when he's finished. I open my eyes to see him rummaging through a drawer under the basin and coming out with a hair claw clip. He sticks it between his teeth and sweeps up my hair, twisting it up and holding it in place with the clip.

"Thanks," I murmur.

"Can you manage the rest on your own?" he asks quietly.

I lower my eyes and accept the help he is offering. I shake my head.

"Get out," he says, turning to the other men. "Go and wait in the kitchen."

I almost weep with relief. I didn't want to stand here naked and vulnerable in front of all of them, but I simply cannot do this by myself. Layton helps me off the stool as the other men leave.

"Wait," I say, stopping them in their tracks. "Before you go, I need you all to know something. He—he..." I stop and inhale deeply, gathering my inner strength. "He wore a condom," I blurt out before I lose my nerve.

Declan hisses and growls. "I fucking killed him."

My eyes shoot to his. "Sm-Smith?"

He nods grimly.

Oddly, that makes me feel slightly stronger. For the first time in what feels like forever, I smile. I knew that Declan would take care of this for me. I knew he would look out for me in the only way he could at the time. How he knew it was him, I guess he will tell me when he's ready.

I nod and they leave me and Layton alone.

"May I?" Layton asks, his hands, hovering near the hem of the jersey.

I nod.

He steps into the shower, getting completely drenched now and carefully gets my arms free first and then grips the hem, gently lifting it over my head.

My heart is thundering in my chest. I want to hide. I want to cover up and disappear, but there is no need. Layton avoids looking at me as he grabs the soap and sponge and slowly gets to work. He lifts my left arm up first and I recoil from the smell of B.O. I'm so embarrassed but he doesn't even flinch. He just cleans me up and then sets to work on my other stinky pit. I let out a muffled moan when he rubs the sponge over the sites of the injections that Boomer issued. He stops instantly.

"I see," he murmurs, but doesn't probe me for information.

He leaves my upper arms alone and skates over the thin scratch at my throat and then down in between my breasts. I'm frozen in place when he runs the sponge under them, but it's over quickly and I breathe out slowly.

He steps back. "I will steady you if you want to do the rest yourself," he says.

"It's okay," I murmur and grab his wrist to help me off the

stool.

"Are you sure?" he asks.

I nod and part my legs slightly.

He takes the soap and lathers it up before he drops it on the dish and carefully rubs his hand between my legs. I let out a whimper and he whips his hand away quickly, but I shake my head. "I'm okay. Please, get rid of the feel of him."

"Fuck, Ruby," he mutters, but it's the only sign of emotion from him. He has detached himself from this situation and isn't looking at me like the woman he is involved with, but rather someone he needs to clean and take care of. I fall in love with him in that moment harder and faster than I ever thought possible. There is no pressure, no intimidation, no need for me to apologize for flinching or thank him for being gentle.

When it's all over, he steps out of the shower soaking wet, but only grabs one towel. I help out and turn the taps off before he wraps me in the black fluffy towel, cradles me in his arms and carries me to the bedroom, where he proceeds to dry me off and wrap me in a soft robe, avoiding putting any pressure on the wound.

"Are you hungry?" he asks, breaking the silence, after drying himself as best he can. "Ramsey's making soup."

"Is that what I can smell?" I ask and ignore my growling stomach.

He lets out a soft laugh and holds his hand out for me. "I'll take that as a yes."

I let him lead me slowly out of the bedroom and towards the kitchen where I will need every ounce of fortitude I have to face the four men as not my caregivers any longer, but as my lovers, after I've killed a man, was abducted, tortured, stabbed, raped, killed *another* man and finally made it back to them with my soul destroyed, my body battered, bruised and my mind slightly broken.

Chapter Seven

Ruby

I let go of Layton's hand the moment we enter the kitchen. I don't need him to help me anymore. I'm going to show them all that I'm okay, or as okay as I can be and that I don't need to be coddled over.

"Rubes," David says. "What can I get you?"

I roll my eyes at him. "What are you? Head waiter today? I'll get my own damn coffee from my own damn kitchen."

He grins at me and leaves me to stagger slowly to the coffee pot. I grimace at it, knowing I have to reach up into the cupboard for a mug, but I'm doing it by myself come hell or high water.

Slowly, I extend my arm over my head to open the cupboard. The stitches in my wound protest vigorously, but I press my lips together and carry on. I feel the sweat forming under my arms again and I'm annoyed that Layton's job of freshening me up is going to waste. The kitchen is silent. My hand starts to shake as I grip the mug and pull it out of the cupboard.

Come on, Rubes. You are being stubborn. Let them help you.

No.

Okay, you know it's bad when the voices in your head have conversations with each other.

Against my will, the shaking gets worse and the mug slips from my fingers to shatter on the Italian tile of the kitchen floor, like a gunshot going off.

I gasp and drop my arm, clutching at my side.

"Dammit, Ruby," Declan growls, as David rushes over to clear up the mess.

"You've cut yourself," David murmurs, running the back of his finger over my bare and bleeding foot.

"I'm okay," I snap.

"No, you are a pig-headed woman who needs to learn that she isn't alone anymore," Declan says, smugly reaching for a mug with ease and pouring me a hot coffee.

Okay, he isn't smug, that is me projecting but still. Not fair. I should be able to take care of myself.

I let him lead me to the small table, and I sit down in relief. I accept the mug with a tight smile, which probably came across more like a scowl, judging by Declan's annoying smirk.

"Before anyone says anything, there's some things I need to say," I start after taking a small sip. I place the mug down and wrap my cold hands around it.

"First off, thank you for taking care of me. I know I am a burden, and as soon as I can pour out my own fucking coffee, you don't have to hover over me anymore."

"Ruby," Ramsey says, but I shush him.

"Let me get this out, please."

He nods and shuts up.

"I'm going to tell you exactly what happened to me and

then I never, and I mean *never* want to talk or hear about it again. Is that clear?"

"Whatever you need," David murmurs.

I nod and look down at my coffee. I start at the beginning with sneaking out of the front door of the club and heading in the Uber to Perfect Ten's. I tell them about the conversation with Jake, the recording and then killing him. I tell them about finding a stranger in the Uber and him knocking me out. I whisper the words about how I woke up half naked, and what Boomer did to me and his revelation about my parents. I stammer my way through the stabbing and the rape. I practically yell at them with how I killed Boomer and then I'm done.

Exhausted, and emotionally battered and bruised.

"Oh, love," David murmurs and crouches down next to me. "You are so strong to be able to tell us all of that. We love you."

I give him a brief shaky smile and then take another sip of my now cold coffee.

"I need to get away for a while," I say after a beat. "I think I'll go back to my parents' house, just for a bit."

"You said you'd come to Ireland with me," Declan says slowly. "I was hoping we could go there as soon as you are back on your feet."

I swallow. I hadn't forgotten and I'd kind of hoped he'd say that. I just didn't want to ask and sound all needy, or like I was desperate to go to his family home and meet his mom. I didn't want him to read too much into it.

"Okay," I say, after pretending to think about it for a few seconds. "That'll be nice for a few days."

He shakes his head. "No, Ruby. I was thinking more like a few weeks or months even."

I frown. "No, I can't do that. I can't leave Manchester for

an extended period. I have my business and my empire here will crumble like a fresh cookie if I'm not here to defend it."

"I get that, but, Ruby, we've kicked up a massive stink around here in the last few days. What with the explosion on the Industrial Estate, Jake's murder, the fire on the outskirts of town, not to mention *Smith's*," he growls the name and I flinch, "disappearance. He may have been as crooked as they come, but he was still a copper. We need to get out of the city, out of the country for an indefinite period."

"Don't worry about your business," David says. "Let them take it."

I snarl at him, but he waves his hand dismissively. "We will go to Ireland, you will heal and come back stronger than ever and then we can come back here and reclaim everything and more."

I take in his words and then smile. He's learning how this life works.

"Okay, then," I say, but make sure to put contingencies in place. No way am I leaving my city to get taken over. "When do we leave?"

"Tomorrow," Declan says. "If that's not too soon for you?"

I shake my head and haul my sorry ass to my feet. "I'll prepare," I say and hobble painfully to the door. I pause and without looking back, I say, "I'm saying this to everyone except Declan. I have killed. Not once, not twice, not three times. More than half a dozen times in the last six years. That's what my life is. If you can't handle that or knowing this makes you think less of me, I need you to speak out now before I fall deeper into this relationship."

Silence.

Then the three men I addressed, quickly come to me with words of reassurance. Even David.

"We are not going anywhere," he says, "none of us. We are all in this together now. We love you."

I nod and then clench my fist. I have something that needs doing. Something I desperately need to heal my fractured mind.

"Daddy," I say quietly. "I need to confess my sins and be absolved."

You could hear a pin drop a thousand miles away.

Chapter Eight

Declan

"You have got to be kidding me," I hiss at her, striding closer and wanting to shake some sense into her.

"Do I look like I'm joking?" she asks in a tone that is completely devoid of any emotion. She turns from us and walks away, in the direction of her bedroom, fully expecting me to follow her.

I do, but only to inform her that Daddy isn't coming out to play today, or for a while for that matter.

The other men silently follow, probably also wondering if she has lost her mind.

I find her in the bedroom, standing at the foot of the big white bed, staring over it at the painting above the headboard. It's Impressionist and I don't have a fucking clue what it is meant to be of. But it's her focus, so I look at it a bit harder.

"I'm not doing anything to hurt you," I say quietly. I can't yell at her, not now. Quiet force is the way to go here.

"Bring the box out from under the bed," she says, ignoring me.

I give Layton a death stare when he does as she asks. What the fuck is he doing encouraging this?

He lays it on the bed and opens it.

"Take out the cat-o'-nine-tails."

He does.

"Give it to Daddy, please."

"Ruby," I warn her with a tone that would usually work on *anyone* else in the world.

Layton holds it out to me, but I can see his reluctance. He just wants to do what she says, but he isn't happy about it.

"I'm not taking that," I insist, folding my arms over my chest defiantly.

"Yes, you are," David croaks out.

"Excuse me?" I ask incredulously, fixing my death gaze onto him.

He flinches but doesn't back down.

"She is asking you to do this. It is your duty to give her what she needs right now. Do you have to like it? No. None of us do. But it is what Ruby wants," he says softly.

"Ruby has lost her mind," I snarl.

"I'm still here and I'm of perfectly sound mind, if not body," she says. "Do this or I will find someone who will," she adds, cutting me badly.

"Then you find someone else," I state coldly.

She turns her head to look at me. "Do you love me?" she asks.

I hesitate. She's going to pull that one. "You know I do," I mutter.

"Then you will do this," she replies. She turns her body to face me. "Bare my back."

"No," I grit out.

"Do it or we are over, and I don't just mean the role play," she says, her eyes flashing with a warning that I take very seriously. She is a woman who knows her own mind. She knows she needs to be absolved for killing Boomer, but this isn't the way, or the time. I start to shake my head, but the plea that falls into her eyes forces me to close mine so I can't see it. Opening my eyes, with a heavy heart, I step closer to her and loosen the belt of her robe. My steady hands are shaking when I reach up to push it off her shoulders. She catches it by tightening her elbows into her sides so that it doesn't fall completely to the floor.

Then she turns back to face the painting.

I hold my hand out for the whip and Layton drops it lightly against my palm, then he moves across the room to stand with the other men.

"Go," I croak out.

"Stay," she says calmly. "I want you all to witness this."

"Fuck," I moan. "Princess, please."

Silence.

She has nothing left to say and if I don't do this, she will leave me. I don't know which is worse right now. My heart is hammering in my chest when I whisper, "Have you been a bad girl, Princess?"

Her tense shoulders relax, and I see her take a deep breath.

"Yes," she says, exhaling slowly.

I shuffle around so that I'm facing her back. I can see our initials etched into her skin by Layton the other night.

"What have you done?" I ask, forcing my voice to steady out.

"I have betrayed the men I care about," she whispers. "The men that I lo—love."

I cast my glance to the other three men, who aren't moving a muscle. No. This is all on me. I feel sick.

"How so?" I ask.

"I let another man touch me," she says.

"No," I say, shaking my head vehemently. "Ruby. No!"

"I allowed another man inside me. I betrayed the men I love."

"Dammit," I shout at her. "What are you doing?"

Nothing.

I pull my arm back and whip her as lightly as I can, knowing she will only say it again and again and I can't hear it. My stomach clenches into a tight ball.

"Harder," she murmurs.

"No."

"Harder. I fucked another man," she spits out harshly.

"Ruby!"

"Harder, Daddy. I need this."

"Fuck!" I roar at her and whip her again, this time a bit harder. I know exactly how to wield this fucking instrument. I know exactly how much force to use to not hurt her and how much force will break the skin.

"Again," she says steadily.

Feeling the bile rise in my throat, I do as she asks.

She doesn't utter a single sound. She just stands there.

"Anything else, Princess?" I croak out.

"I killed a man," she says.

I whip her harder this time. It jolts her body, but I'm still being as gentle as I can. Much more and I will hurt her, and I would rather lose her forever than do that.

"Did he deserve it?"

"Yes, but it doesn't change the fact that he is dead, and I killed him."

I whip her again, making sure to angle the tails as far away from the letters on her back as I can.

"You are a bad girl," I murmur.

"I know," she says. "Can you forgive me, Daddy?"

"Of course," I croak out.

I lift the whip one last time and this time, I strike her with enough force to mark her exquisite skin. If I don't, she won't feel as if she has been punished.

"Again," she whispers. "Please, Daddy. Absolve me of these sins."

I close my eyes and lash her back again and then again before I drop my arm to my side. I inhale slowly and then I take two steps to stand next to her, facing her as she stares blankly at the wall.

"If you ever ask me to do something like this again, Princess, it will be *my* decision to leave. Do you understand me?"

She turns her head slowly. It rips my heart out when I see the unshed tears pooled in her beautiful green eyes. But they aren't tears of pain or torment or fear. It's liberation. "Understood, Daddy," she says and looks back at the wall.

I fling the whip onto the bed in front of her and storm out of the room, shoving David aside and catching a glimpse of Ramsey with his fist to his mouth, looking as if he is about to vomit. I understand that feeling.

I need to get away from her. I need air. I can't breathe.

Stumbling out of the back door into the garden, I try to catch my breath. My head is spinning, and I want to crawl into a hole and die for what I've just done to her. What she just made me do.

"It's okay," David's voice breaks through the thunder in my ears. "She's okay. You did the right thing."

"Did I?" I growl at him. "That's easy for you to say. *You* didn't just punish her for being raped, for the love of fuck. Why? Why did she want me to do that?"

"I'm new to all of this," David says quietly. "I don't fully understand the dynamic of this relationship you have with her, but I do know that she needed this. She is more at peace now. Go to her and you'll see."

I shake my head. "I should've called her bluff. I should've refused."

David snorts. "Yeah, nope. Ruby doesn't make idle threats. You'd have been out on your arse quicker than the speed of light."

"Well, *I* don't make idle threats either. She *ever* asks me to do anything even remotely like that again, I'm out of here."

"Liar," David says lightly.

I turn to him with a hiss of rage intending to punch him, but instead I draw back and throw my fist at the wall as hard as I can. Then I do it again.

"Stop that," David says. "I've already cleaned your hand up once, now I've got to do it again."

"Who asked you to?"

He shrugs and I search his hazel eyes. They are so full of light. There isn't even a speck of darkness showing in them yet.

I reach out and to his surprise, I cup his face. "Keep being that annoying ball of sunshine for her. She needs you to be that for her. I want to be her everything but I'm just a cold, depraved *killer* swamped in a pitch-black filth that is bad for her. So very bad for her. Promise me, you won't let the darkness touch you, David."

"I promise," he murmurs.

I nod and with the rage and frustration and *pain* of loving Ruby so much, it physically hurts me, I drop my hand to David's throat, and I shove him up against the wall. I plant my lips on his in a kiss driven by fear and lust and heartache. His tongue touching mine sparks up a tiny bit of light, the light that burns for Ruby, but is currently choking under the smog of disgust I feel at myself for doing what I did to her. I don't think I can ever forgive myself for absolving her of being violated. It makes me sick to my stomach. I won't be able to look her in the eye for a while, nor myself in the mirror.

I am nothing but filth.

I don't deserve her.

I pull back from the kiss, panting slightly. I don't know if Ruby would approve of us kissing out here while she lies in bed, in pain and anguish. All I know is that even though I am no good for her, I can't stay away from her. It is now my turn to ask for *her* forgiveness on my hands and knees... and hope that she bestows it on me, or I will be forever lost to the black hole that she pulled me back from, even when she didn't know me.

Chapter Nine

Ruby

Sitting at the vanity opposite the bed, I don't want to look at myself just yet. I have my eyes firmly closed while Layton rubs a warm, soothing lavender scented oil onto my back. Daddy didn't hurt me that much. I know he couldn't. I could see it on his face that he felt sick doing what I asked, but the important thing is, he *did* what I asked. I really didn't think he would.

"Better," I murmur. My bones and muscles are aching from the trauma, and this is helping my whole being.

"Here," Layton mutters and steps away from me.

I feel a cool touch and I open my eyes, aiming them where I think Declan's face will appear in the mirror.

He is pale, grim-faced and pissed off, but he gently takes over the aftercare, and it makes me smile slightly to myself.

"Thank you," I murmur, closing my eyes again.

"Don't," he says shortly. "Do not thank me for this."

"I needed it..." I start, but he hisses and interrupts me.

"I get that, but you have to respect that it hurt me to do this, and I only did it because you threatened me into it."

"I know," I say lightly.

"I meant what I said," he grouses. "Ask me to do something like this again and I will walk."

"I don't believe you, but if something like this *ever* happens again, you can just go ahead and kill me because I don't think I can survive a third round."

"Jesus," he mutters. "Ruby." His hands go still on my back and then he moves around to sit on the vanity to look down at me. "Don't ever joke about that."

"Who's joking?" I ask with a shrug.

"You will never give up, do you hear me?" he says as gently as he can with his face contorted in agony.

"I know it hurts you," I whisper. "I know it hurts all of you, but…"

"No," he says. "I will never let you get to that point. I will never let you be hurt again."

"You can't promise that," I say reasonably. "You can't watch me twenty-four seven."

"Wanna bet?" he growls and then drops to his knees to take my hand lightly, allowing me to pull back if I need to.

I don't.

I don't feel threatened or intimidated or scared of him in any way. None of them, in fact. In the short time that we have been involved, they have proven themselves to me in ways that are unfathomable and quite frankly, startling. It took me years to trust anyone with my body after the first time. I'm scared that it will take me as long now and they will leave me.

"Forgive me?" Declan asks, interrupting my thoughts.

"Always," I murmur. "Besides, there's nothing to forgive. I asked you to do something for me and despite not wanting to, you did it. For me. Where's David? I have something to say."

"I'm here," he says, entering the room, looking a little sheepish.

I narrow my eyes at his flushed face and then my eyes wander over to Declan with a soft smirk. "You two get up to something outside?"

"We kissed," Declan says straight away. "I initiated it and when it occurred to me that perhaps you would not be happy about it, I ended it."

"Why do you think I wouldn't be happy about it?" I ask, my issue tabled for a moment. I'm intrigued by this development and not in the least bit jealous or angry about it. In fact, the opposite. I think it's hot and sexy and they are going to need each other in the coming days in ways that maybe just a friendship won't suffice.

"It was behind your back," Declan says.

"Not really. You did more than kiss the other night. I am under the assumption it wasn't a one-off," I try to keep the question out of my voice.

David remains completely silent. He has deferred to Declan in this matter and that also intrigues me seeing as Declan is a novice in this area by his own admission, whereas David has the experience.

"Noo," Declan says slowly, drawing it out, "but to be honest, I hadn't thought about it after everything that happened. The kiss outside was driven by solace and fear and self-loathing. Uhm, no offense, Sunshine," he adds to David, who snickers.

"None taken. I figured as much," he says.

"Is it something you wish to pursue? Both of you?" I want to hear from David. Need to hear. I need consent on both sides and for one or the other to not feel pressured. Not ever, but especially not now.

"Yes," David says first. "If Declan wants to."

"I do," Declan says. "It was liberating and, I can't explain it very well, but it felt right. Right time, right person..." He trails off with a thoughtful expression. "However," he adds. "I don't think I want a separate relationship." He looks at David. "Whatever happens, it happens with Ruby. Is that okay with you?"

David nods. "Of course. I was of the same mind."

"Great," I chirp and then sigh. "But I need to say something now that you are all here." I turn painfully and wearily on the dresser stool, and take in Ramsey near the bed, Layton standing guard at the door, David perched on the bed and Declan leaning against the vanity.

"I know what you're going to say, and it's not necessary," Layton says. "We are here regardless of anything else."

"I know that, but this relationship is so new. We have only been together as a whole *once*. I—I'm not sure when I will be able to—to have s—sex again. It doesn't mean that I don't love you all. I do. In different ways. I wasn't sure about love. I never thought I would be able to love anyone or that anyone would or *could* love me. Past relationships, if you could even call them that, were always about what I got out of it. What they did for me. Anyone who wanted to date me for my business was told where to go. I am not ready to say the words to you all. I don't know when I will say them, and I don't know when I will be able to give my body to you again. If—if that is a deal breaker, then I completely understand." I take shallow breaths, my eyes lowered.

"Ruby," David says. "Look at me."

I raise my eyes to his. "Layton has already said it wasn't necessary to say any of that. We understand completely. There is no pressure here. None at all. If you never want to have sex again, we don't care. We are here for you, and we will take our cues from you. As for saying you love us, what you've just said is everything. We don't need to hear the rest."

I nod, not being able to say anything for fear of choking on the sob that is threatening to explode out of me.

I give them all as much of a smile as I can muster and then after a steadying breath, I say, "I'm tired. Would you mind leaving me alone to rest now?"

"Of course," Ramsey says, approaching me with caution and holding his hand out to help me up.

"Let me do it myself," I murmur, and he drops his hand without protest.

He bends to kiss the top of my head and then he leaves, with David.

When he reaches the door, Declan says, "We will be here when you wake up. Rest, Princess. We've got you."

I nod my thanks.

Layton turns to leave, but I say, "Wait."

He pauses, his blue eyes meeting mine filled with curiosity.

I reach out and shove the small black pouch that was left on the vanity in plain sight. I know what's in there and it's time to capitulate. There is no way I can rest up enough to get on my feet tomorrow to go to Ireland with the pain I'm in right now.

"You sure?" he asks.

I nod. "I'm trusting you," I whisper. "All of you, not to leave me."

"Never," he says, taking two giant steps towards me and dropping to his knees. He takes my hands and kisses them. "You have four men here who will die for you, sweetheart. You don't have to be afraid to rest."

Swallowing, I lean forward and press my lips to his forehead before pulling back quickly. It's as much intimate contact as I can stomach right now.

"Jab my ass?" I ask with a laugh that I summon up from fuck knows where in my dark soul.

He chuckles. "Anytime," he replies and picks up the pouch, unzipping it.

"Let me get on the bed and close my eyes. I can't see them. I just...can't."

He stands up and steps back, letting me haul my battered body up by myself so I can hobble to the bed. I sink onto it with such relief it makes my head spin. I scrunch my eyes closed and tense up when Layton gently pushes me over slightly and lifts up my robe. It's over with before I know it. He didn't warn me. He just did it. And I appreciate it more than words can say.

"Thanks," I mutter and unscrunch my eyes, but keep them closed so I can sleep. "What you did to your arm..." I mumble.

"Yeah?"

"I love it."

He pulls the covers over me and kisses my forehead and then he leaves, closing the door behind him.

The fear of being alone and vulnerable is squashed by the morphine and soon I'm lulled into a sleep, knowing that if nothing else, I'm not really on my own. I have people who care about me and will keep me safe now.

Chapter Ten

Ramsey

"She didn't eat anything," I say, slumped in the armchair at the end of the fancy glass coffee table.

"She will when she's ready", David says, holding his phone to his ear.

Mine beeps next to me for a message and I glance at it out of something to do. Squinting at it, I scowl and drop it on the arm of the chair again.

"Problem?" David asks.

"Nope," I say and look away. "Who are you trying to get hold of?" I ask to deflect. I do not want to discuss the text that the hospice has just sent me. Yeah, it seems harsh to send a death notification by text, but I told them under no circumstances to ring me. Ever. I'm not interested in speaking to them and hearing how sorry they are that my bitch mother has finally been dragged down to hell.

"The Banker," David replies. "It's a system..." He waves his hand dismissively.

"What for?" I ask. I've heard about this Banker guy. He is

the one that runs the off-the-record books for all of Ruby's Underworld businesses and apparently goes round collecting protection money from local businesses in Ruby's turf.

"You think I meant what I said about leaving her business to the hyaenas?" he scoffs. "Please. We have worked too damn hard to lose it all. The Banker will watch it and make sure no one makes a move on her ground."

I snort. "Sneaky. I like it. Can't say I want to come back to find my job has been handed to some bell-end who works for Scott."

"Speaking of Scott…what are we going to do about him?" David asks.

"*We* aren't going to do anything," Declan pipes up from his post of staring out of the window over the back garden. "It's taken care of."

"Meaning?" I ask, sitting forward and resting my elbows on my knees.

"Meaning, it's taken care of," he says and then pulls his vibrating phone out of his pocket. He looks at it and declines the call. That's the sixth time I've seen him do this in the last couple of days.

"We keeping you from something?" I jibe.

"It's nothing," he says.

"Finally," David grouses into the phone. "Listen up…"

I tune him out as he wanders off into the kitchen and pick up my own phone to stare at the message again.

I sigh. I won't respond to it. They can burn her body and throw her in the bin for all I care. I'm not getting involved. Too much pain, too much of her shit to put up with over the years. As I got older, into my early teens, I spent more and more time at Layton's house or over at Pete Wilson's. His mum was nice, and we used to talk. Pete's dad had left a while ago and I think she was lonely. It wasn't until much later on that I realized she took advantage of me. I was just a kid and she seduced me. Oh, I was all Billy Big Spuds about it at the time, but now I just feel sad that my first time wasn't with someone I cared about. Still, she gave me what I needed at the time.

"Hey," Layton says. "There's an Uber on its way to take you back to your place so you can pick up a few things for the trip."

"I don't want to leave Ruby," I protest.

"We'll go in shifts. You can't arrive there with only the clothes on your back."

"Fine," I grouse. I don't see why I have to go first. Although, in hindsight, if I go now while Ruby is still sleeping, I'll be back when she wakes up. "Where are we staying?" I ask, the thought just occurring to me.

"David's organizing it," Declan says. "For feck's sake," he adds under his breath as his phone goes off again.

"Just answer the fucking thing, would you?" I snap at him.

He turns to give me a death stare. I raise my chin a little, not intimidated by the cold-blooded killer one bit. If he wants to start, I'm more than ready.

"It's about a job," he grits out. "I'm not leaving Ruby, so I'm not taking it."

"Oh," I murmur and suppress the shudder. I haven't really had much chance to think about what he does for a living. He must be ice-cold to be able to separate that from his normal life. Whatever his normal life is. So far, we haven't seen much of anything apart from him being with Ruby. I guess seeing him with his mum will shed some light onto the man, and not the killer. "Hey, do you have siblings?" I ask as the thought pops into my head.

"Yes," he replies and then stalks out of the sitting room, in a definite move to avoid me asking more questions.

"Well, okay, then," I murmur.

Layton snickers. "He won't be able to keep it secret much longer."

"True. Mum's died," I blurt out, needing to get it out there to the one person who knows how much I don't give a shit.

"Oh," he says and leaves it at that, knowing I don't want to add anything.

With that said, I pick up my phone and delete the text, in a way, deleting that woman from my life at the same time.

"How are we going to make sure Ruby is taken care of?" I ask quietly, worrying about whether we can be everything she needs.

"It's simple," Declan says, returning with David. "If she wants to work, David gives her work to do. If she wants to go on a picnic in the park, Ramsey you take her. If she wants to just sit and stare into space, Layton, you sit with her and if she needs someone to end up in a world of hurt, I'll take care of it. And then, when all of that is over, we gather her close and let her know that no matter what she wants, or what she needs, one of us will be able to give it to her. We all love her, but we have specific skill sets. We use them for her individual needs. The rest…will fall into place."

"You sound really sure about that," I say.

"I've seen her fight through this once before when she was younger and weaker. She will make this pain her bitch before long and bounce back stronger than ever. When that happens, we will take back everything she has lost and the Underworld had better watch out because she will take no prisoners," he says.

"What about her parents? Shouldn't we tell them…something?" I ask.

"If you want to ring Rex up and inform him of everything that has happened to his daughter, then be my guest. I, personally, will be staying well out of that. Rex will burn the world down for his girl and trust me, you don't want to get caught up in the crossfire."

"Noted," I murmur. "I hope she knows that we would also burn the world down for her."

"She knows," David says. "She knows."

Chapter Eleven

Ruby

My eyes flutter open. My ceiling swims into view and I blink a couple of times. I turn my head to the window to see that it's night out. I must not have slept for very long. I sigh and struggle to sit up from my position propped up on the pillows behind me. I swing my legs gingerly over the side of the bed and reach out to turn the lamp on. I smile when I see a brand-new phone lying on the nightstand.

"You are a gem," I mutter and pick it up. I'm startled when I see that it is the next day. I've slept for about twenty-four hours. Dammit. That means we've missed our flight. But I must've needed the rest, or I wouldn't have slept that long. I place my phone back on the nightstand and with sorrow, mourn the loss of my knives. My pretty, pretty knives that have saved my life more than once. I sigh and open the drawer to pull out the bottle of painkillers when my heart stops and tears spring to my eyes.

"Fuck," I murmur and pull out two brand new knives and holsters. "How did I get so lucky to have met all of you?"

I stroke them lovingly and then replace them carefully in the drawer. I pop two pills and gulp them down with a bottle of water. I gave in to the pain earlier, but I won't again. I force myself to my feet with as little help as possible. I'm going into my third day of this wound and by fuck, I'm not going to let it slow me down any more than is humanly possible. Inhaling, I take a step towards the door and then another and then it becomes easier. I open the door and nearly jump out of my skin.

"Jesus!" I shriek when I see Declan sitting on the floor, legs stretched out, right outside my door.

He smiles up at me and rises gracefully. "How do you feel?" he asks.

"Better," I say, meaning it. All that rest did me the world of good. "Hungry," I add when I can smell food close by.

"Thought so," he says and holds his arm out for me to take.

I do, linking mine through his and we walk slowly but steadily to the kitchen.

"Soup and homemade bread?" I ask. "Which kitchen god is responsible for this?"

"Me," Ramsey says, holding his hand up like a schoolboy.

I giggle. "Handy man to have around, aren't you?"

"Dude's got skills," David says lightly. "Did you see your new phone?"

"I did. Thank you."

He grins, pleased with himself.

"And the knives?" Layton asks.

I nod. "Very pretty," I murmur.

Declan leads me to the table, and I sit down. Ramsey produces a bowl of steaming hot soup and delicious warm bread and I don't even care that I slurp and gobble it all up like a woman starved for many days. Which I suppose I am.

When I'm finished, I sit back, replete and smile. It's shaky, but it's real. "You are all amazing. I'm sorry I slept so long, and we missed our flight."

"Don't be," Declan says. "It's a private jet. It will wait."

"Oh?" I ask, and then a sense of dread fills me. "You didn't borrow it from my mom, did you?" I ask with trepidation. If *any* of these men went to my parents, I'll gut them with my brand-new rainbow-colored switchblade.

Declan scoffs. "If you think I'm eejit enough to say anything about this to your da, then you don't think very highly of me."

I relax. "Phew," I joke, wiping my brow.

"Princess, please give us a little bit of credit," he says, but shoots Ramsey a look that speaks volumes.

I raise my eyebrow, but clearly, they haven't violated my privacy. I hate that I can't tell them, but there is no way they would let this lie.

"What about Scarlet?" David asks, and then purses his lips when he gives Declan a filthy look. "Should we tell her what's gone on?"

"Don't look at him that way," I chide David. "He did nothing wrong. But no. I don't want any of my family to know. Scar will worry and tell Mom, and then Rex will find out and, well…" I make an explosion motion with my hands.

He nods. "Your pyro friend called, by the way. He's good to go."

I nod and then bite my lip. "We definitely need to get out of town as soon as possible," I say unnecessarily.

"As soon as you're ready," Declan says.

I nod. "Give me some time to pack," I say and stand up, with help from the table.

"Ah, skills," David says, knowingly and holds his arm out for me. "I've got this."

I give them all a curious look, wondering what on earth is going on, but take his arm and let him lead me back to the bedroom.

"Bathroom," I murmur and pull away so that I can, hopefully, pee in peace this time.

When I return, David is sorting through all my clothes, having dragged a suitcase out from under the bed.

I lower myself to the bed and watch him, barely needing to give any input whatsoever. He knows me. He knows what I need, and soon he has neatly and efficiently packed a suitcase with enough clothes for a week. Declan has reassured me that Mama Gannon will allow me use of her washing machine and tumble dryer, so I'm happy with David's selection.

"We can leave in a couple of hours," Declan says, coming off his phone from rearranging the flight. "Why don't you rest for another hour and then we'll start getting you ready. It's going to be an arduous journey in your condition. And I don't mean that in any other way than fact," he adds before I can blast him from all sides.

I chuckle and lie back on the pillows. "Fine," I grouse and then it comes out of the blue, sideswiping me with a force that makes my body convulse as I gulp for air, and feel the walls closing in on me.

Chapter Twelve

Ruby

Layton steps forward and gently pushes me off the pillows as I struggle to take my next breath.

Panic attack.

I know these well. I thought I had gotten rid of them years ago, but apparently, they were just dormant, lying-in wait for the opportunity to make a comeback.

Layton rubs my back and murmurs words that I can't hear through the roaring of blood in my ears. The more I can't breathe, the worse it becomes. I panic through the panic attack, flailing my arms about as all the air leaves my lungs and there is none to inhale.

"It's okay, sweetheart," Layton whispers. "We've got you."

"T-tell me,' I gasp, whacking Declan on the head as I try to grab him, but I've lost all ability to control my limbs. "T-ell me…he-he's d-dead," I splutter.

"He is very dead, Princess," Declan says grimly. "I shot him in the head and burned his body."

"Again," I pant as the air I need to breathe suddenly reappears in minute doses. My breathing is ragged. I'm still struggling. I feel sick and lightheaded, but I'm coming back.

"I shot out both of his knees and then shot him in the head before I burned his body," he says, leaning in closer to me. "He is dead, Princess. I killed him and he can never hurt you again."

"Again," I rasp.

He repeats it over and over again until I feel myself able to draw air into my lungs properly. I nod erratically, taking it in. Accepting it. He wouldn't lie to me. I trust him.

"Promise me," I whisper.

He takes my hand and links our fingers together. "I promise you, Princess. He is gone. He can never hurt you again."

I close my eyes and moan, hating this weakness, this *vulnerability*. But I can't stop it. Tears well up and pour out of my eyes. I turn into Layton's chest, and he wraps his arms around me, stroking my hair and kissing my head.

"Let it all out, sweetheart," he says. "We are all here for you."

My body, wracked with my sobbing, hurts. I've pulled my stitches and I know I'm bleeding, but I don't care. I need to cry. I need to have this night to be vulnerable, to ask for reassurance, to be weak. Tomorrow, I won't let this affect me ever again. I don't want it to. I hate this feeling. Tomorrow, I'm going to push it aside, bury it deep, chain it up and let it keep my other demons company. Tomorrow, this ends.

But tonight, I need to cry.

I quieten down at some point. I have no idea how long it took me. But Michelle is here now and pulling me gently away from my big, comforting man and helping me lay down so she can examine the damage I've done to my stitches. Her ripping the bandage off is the worst part. I moan and go lightheaded, even more so if that's possible, but then I just feel nothing. That area is numb, and I curse.

"Damn you. I said no needles," I hiss.

"Tough," she replies. "You can pretend to be the big bad all you like out there, but in here you are *my* bitch, and you do as *I* say. Got it?"

"Uhm," I murmur, only slightly surprised by her attitude. I mean she is a crooked doctor; she has to have some balls. "What do you mean *pretend*?" I ask, insulted.

David snickers, but then goes pale when he looks at the wound and Michelle re-sewing it up.

"It's not that bad," she says. "These are dissolvable so the first lot should be gone in a couple of days. Take it easy, Ruby. Please. Your body has been through a lot."

I nod and feel bad for making her do more work on me. Then I remember how much her monthly retainer is for shit like this, and the guilt dissipates.

She finishes up and replaces the sticky bandage. "You can take that off in about three days' time, or I can come back and do it."

"We won't be here," I mutter. "I can handle it."

She narrows her eyes. "You shouldn't travel…"

"Save it," I snap. "We can't stay here. *I* can't stay here. We're going, end of story."

"Okay," she says, holding her hands up in defeat. "But please tell me you have someone where you are going who can check you over next week?"

"Covered," Declan says to my surprise. Although why I'm surprised is a mystery. He is as far underground as I am. He knows people.

"Good," Michelle says and then stands up. "Call me when you get back."

I nod and watch as Layton walks her out.

"Can you help me get dressed," I ask him when he returns a few moments later.

"No, Ruby, you need to rest," Declan says. "We can push the flight back again."

"No, we can't. I *need* to get out of here. Please?" I can feel the walls closing in again, but this time, I push them back. I'm not falling into that pit of despair again. I refuse.

"Okay," he says with a grim nod at all the reminders of why we have to get out of dodge A-SAP. "Layton, help her."

Layton gives him a glare before he helps me to my feet. I wince and hobble to the bathroom where my super sweet giant of a man takes care of me for what I hope will be the final time in this way.

Chapter Thirteen

Ruby

About forty-five minutes later, we are well on our way to the airport. I'm sitting in the back of a black Range Rover Evoque, which has appeared out of nowhere and belongs to Declan. He has more cars than he must know what to do with. I'm sitting gingerly on the passenger window side with poor Ramsey squashed in the middle and David on his other side. I wanted it this way and no one was willing to argue with me about it. The reason being, there is something bothering Ramsey, apart from my trauma, and I want to talk to him about it.

"Wanna tell me what's up?" I ask him, picking my moment. It's good to focus on something else.

"Nothing," he says evasively, which just confirms my suspicions.

"You can tell me," I say.

He exhales through his nose, his mouth pressed into a grim line. "My mom died. It's no big deal."

I blink, wondering if I heard him right. "Your mom?" I ask. "I'm so sorry."

"Don't be," he says shortly. "She was a cow and I'm glad she's gone."

Wow. That's cold. If it was my mom, I'd be devastated.

"Still, it must hurt a little."

"Nope."

Okay, this conversation is going nowhere. I ponder whether to pursue it or not for a few moments when he blurts out.

"Look, my childhood sucked shit. I don't like to think about it. I definitely don't like to dwell on it. She's gone and that's that."

"Understood," I murmur.

He turns to look at me. "I wasn't shouting at *you*. I'm just...frustrated and there's this stupid feeling of guilt that I don't care, but it's not enough to make me care...I'm not explaining it right."

"No, I get it," I say. "You do whatever you need to."

He gives me a soft smile. "Thanks."

"If you ever *want* to talk about it, though. I'm here."

"I know." He takes my hand gently, giving me the opportunity to pull back if I need to.

I don't.

We sit in silence for the rest of the journey, and soon we are queuing for yet another checkpoint.

"Shit," Layton mutters, but Declan doesn't fluster or start to panic.

He just rolls down his window and says, "Evening."

The Constable bends down to look at all of us crammed in the back. I sincerely hope he doesn't ask us to get out because I'm fairly sure I can't do that without drawing attention to my gut wound.

"Where you off to?" the Constable asks.

"Ireland," Declan says.

"Passports." Declan hands them all over, having anticipated this and asked for them all before we left the house.

I grimace. Between Declan's fake one and my American one, I hope that we get away without too much suspicion.

I try to relax. The tension is causing my wound to ache.

After several minutes we are ushered through without further comment, and I breathe out in relief.

No one says a word.

It's only when we finally pull up right outside the private jet, an action that I'm over-the-top grateful for, do we start to feel more at ease again.

Only now I'm faced with several steps up into the jet, and I can barely put one foot in front of the other.

I lean heavily on the railing and one foot at a time, make my steady ascent into the cabin. Sinking gratefully into the nearest chair, my hands are shaking and I'm sweating slightly. This is harder than I thought, not just physically, but mentally as well. I thought that I could push it all aside and act like everything is normal, when it's not. It's as far from normal as can be. And I'm not just talking about the abduction and assault. I'm sitting here with *four* men that claim to love me and are happy to be in a relationship as a five-some. I mean, what the fuck? You can't make this stuff up. Seriously. It's mind boggling. The fact that they *still* want to be around me, knowing what happened to me further cements in my mind that they are addled. What if I never want to be intimate again? Can I really expect them to hang around forever waiting, hoping? What kind of selfish bitch does that make me, when they can go off and make a life with someone else? It also raises a very sore subject with me.

Kids.

I don't want them.

I used to.

Before.
Now, I just don't.
Do they?
Do some of them?
What about marriage?
It's not for me.
Do they want that?
Fuck, my head is spinning, and I feel sick.
I close my eyes and groan.

Declan brings me a glass of water, which I take with my eyes still closed and take a sip. "Thanks," I mutter.

"Whatever you need, Princess," he murmurs, taking it from me.

Whatever I need.

Fuck knows what that is right now. I haven't got a fucking clue.

Chapter Fourteen

Ruby

I must've fallen asleep at some point, because I'm jostled awake by Layton picking me up carefully and cradling me.

"I'm awake," I mumble.

"Stay where you are," he murmurs.

I slump against him, but then realize that he is going to struggle to get me down the steps of the aircraft. I wiggle and say, "Put me down, I can walk."

He reluctantly places me on my feet, and I walk unsteadily to the steps where I grip the handrail tightly. The freezing cold Dublin air hits my face, and it wakes me up completely. There is also a light drizzle that makes me glad that Layton put a pair of slip-on sneakers on my feet when he dressed me in casual, loose sweats, a long-sleeved tee and hoodie. I take the slippery steps one at a time, getting irritated that I'm like a toddler, ending up at the bottom in a pissed off mood.

I slide straight into the back of the car unaided, even though I want to scream with agony, and everyone just fits in around me.

The ride to Declan's mom's is glum, but when we get into the neighborhood and he pulls up outside a *very* large and charming home, my mood dissipates. I know that he has bought this for her with the wealth he has accumulated from killing people.

"Wow, nice," I comment, and he chuckles, knowing I've sussed him out. He adores his mom and I love that about him.

It's very late now when Declan grabs my bags from the trunk. I struggle out of the car and finally let Declan help me to the door. Layton takes the keys from Declan before stooping to give me a brief kiss. Ramsey and David do the same, not lingering, just in case.

"I'll see you tomorrow," I whisper, not liking that I have to send them away. It doesn't seem fair, but asking a woman I have never met before to house all of my lovers under her roof is not something I could even contemplate doing. So here we are.

I wave them off and turn back to Declan. He unlocks the door and helps me over the threshold.

"Are you hungry?" he asks.

I shake my head. "Just tired."

He nods and points towards the stairs. Again, I do them one at a time, growling low with frustration, but soon I'm in a beautiful guest room that has been all laid out to perfection for me with fresh flowers, and my own kettle to make tea.

I smile. "She didn't have to do all of this."

"Please," he scoffs. "This is nothing. I had to stop her from putting a Bendicks mint chocolate on your pillow."

I glance over at the pillow. "That's just mean," I joke.

He snickers and drops my bags on the bed. "Do you want me to unpack them?"

I shake my head. "I'll do it in the morning." I sit and toe off my shoes as carefully as I can and then hoist myself further up the bed. "Hope you don't mind if I just crash?" I can't even be bothered to change. It's too much like hard work.

"Of course not. I'll be just down the hall if you need me."

He bends to kiss my head as I give a sleepy yawn. I don't even hear him leave.

* * *

Waking up startled the next morning, I can smell food and my stomach growls. I feel like I could eat a horse, and the jockey with it. I don't even care that I'm still in my sweats from yesterday, I just swing my legs over the side of the bed, wince and stand up.

Stopping in at the bathroom, I make it to the stairs and take them one at a time, gripping the handrail.

"Day four, Rubes, day four," I mutter and follow the aroma towards the kitchen where I find Declan and a very robust, gray-haired woman.

"Ah, you must be Ruby," she says, as soon as she sees me.

Declan sidles over and takes my arm gently, guiding me towards the small round table in the huge kitchen. It's all laid out with the best china and cutlery, and I feel bad she's gone to so much trouble.

"It's lovely to meet you," I murmur, a bit shy. Why? Who the fuck knows? Maybe it's those piercing blue eyes that are boring into my head.

"And you, dear girl. Declan tells me you've had a car accident, and are a bit banged up." She tuts and shakes her head. "Maniacs over there, absolute maniacs."

I stifle my laugh. I'm sure there are also bad Irish drivers, but she wouldn't admit it in a million years, I bet.

"Sure are," I agree, knowing how to keep her on my good side.

She beams and places a platter of bacon, sausages and eggs in front of me to serve myself. I eye it all and wonder if she'd bother if I took it all, but when Declan bites his lip to stop his own laugh, I decide against it.

"Famished," I declare and get another big beam from Mama Gannon.

"I love a woman with a good appetite," she declares, pouring a cup of tea for me. "Remember that girl you used to bring round here, Declan? What was her name again? Anyway, she was as thin as a rail and would only drink boiled water and I never saw her eat more than an apple! What was her name again? She didn't last long."

I give Declan a half smile and ask, "Yes, Declan... what was her name?"

He grimaced at me and replies, "Siobhan."

"Oh, a model, was she?" I ask, my smirk deepening.

"She was," he says, his grimace turning to a glower.

"Yes, well, I hope she stopped all that nonsense and eats like Ruby here now."

I don't take offense in the slightest. The remains of a full Irish breakfast have been presented to me and I waste no time in stabbing a piece of soda bread into my egg yolk and gobbling it.

Mrs. Gannon sits down and pours herself a cup of tea as she continues to talk. Now about someone called *Queever*, I think she said, who is coming for tea tonight so could Declan please watch the stew because Cillian is dropping her off at Bridge this afternoon. I'm excluded from this conversation, luckily, because I'm too busy stuffing my face with glorious home cooked food which, not only lifts my energy levels but my spirit as well. I take another piece of soda bread and wipe it around the plate, soaking up the last of the egg and beans and munch on it before I gulp down the rest of my tea.

"Perfect," Mrs. Gannon says, turning her attention back to me.

"Thank you, Mrs. Gannon," I say politely but she brushes me off.

"Call me Mary, child," she says. "And you're quite welcome. There is nothing more pleasing than someone enjoying the food you've cooked."

"It was delicious, but please don't go to any more trouble for me."

"It's no trouble for you, dear," she says, patting my hand. "Declan, take Ruby into the front room and I'll bring you some tea."

"Any chance of coffee?" I ask, hoping she won't take offense.

"Tea," she says firmly and shoos us out of the kitchen.

"Wait, I'll help clean up," I say, but Declan shakes his head.

"Don't waste your breath. Right now you can do no wrong and she will treat you like the Queen," he says with a laugh.

"Right now?" I ask with a raised eyebrow. "That sounds like you think I'm going to fuck this up."

"Not on your own," he replies. "We still have to tell her about the rest of our relationship."

I give him a look of horror.

"The other men, Ruby, not *that*," he chides me.

I snort and forget for a moment, everything that happened.

But it all rushes back in the next instant and it drains the strength that good food and company gave me.

"Are you okay?" Declan asks straight away, seeing my face fall.

I nod. "Just tired," I lie. "Would your mom mind if I went back upstairs?"

"Of course not, dear," Mary says, bustling into the front room, which is actually a sitting room situated at the front of the house. "Don't mind me. You are here to recuperate. I've left clean towels in your room. Here. Take your tea with you." She tries to hand me the mug, but Declan takes it from her, and with a hand under my elbow, he steers me towards the stairs.

Chapter Fifteen

Ruby

It's sometime later when I wake up from a dead sleep. I haven't slept this much in the previous eight years. I feel groggy and heavy-headed, but I reach for my phone, needing to speak to the other men.

"Hey," I croak when David answers immediately.

"Rubes," he says, the relief flooding his tone. "How's things?" The casual inquiry makes me smile.

"If Mrs. Gannon is going to keep feeding me like she did this morning, I'm going to be the size of this house when we leave. How're all of you?"

"All good," he replies with a smile. "You sound stronger."

"Little bit. I don't feel *as* sore this morning."

"Good, that's good," he says, his voice soft. "Let me put you on speaker."

I smile and chat about the weather and all the dumb things you say when you are trying not to talk about the thing you actually want to talk about. They know it and enable my avoidance like pros.

Ten minutes later, with a promise to get Declan to call them the minute his mom leaves the house so they can come over – cue my teen years in a big way – I hang up and climb off the bed, thinking I really need to get a shower.

I feel capable of doing this myself without any help, so I gather up my freshly laid out towels and my toiletry bag and off I go.

Several painful minutes later, I stagger back to my bedroom, wishing that I wasn't going through this. The only bright spot is knowing that every fucker that I've stabbed in the last eight years, if they got up and walked away, at least they suffered for a few days first before getting on with their lives. With my towel wrapped around my body and my hair wet and tangled, I turn to close the door and see Declan running up the stairs. He stops dead when he sees me, his eyes going to the towel and then shooting back up to mine.

"I need help," I whine, not caring that I feel like a weak bitch for saying so.

"Sure," he says slowly, and approaches me cautiously as if I'm a rabbit about to bolt. "Ruby."

The way he says my name, it's almost as if he is testing it. I scowl at him and turn my back. "Can you untangle this bird's nest on my head, please."

"Mm-hm," he murmurs and takes the brush I shove at him. I sit at the dresser and glare at myself in the mirror. I should be able to reach up and do this myself, but it hurts.

Declan carefully brushes out my hair, doing a thorough job of it in complete silence.

"What's up with you?" I snap at him. "Thinking about Siobhan?"

I prod the bear and quite frankly, I don't give a shit. He is acting weird, and I don't need weird right now. I need normal.

His eyes shoot to mine in the mirror, and he lets out a soft laugh. "Definitely not," he replies.

"Then why are you so pensive?"

He shrugs and leans over me to place the brush back on the dresser.

"Thanks," I mutter and haul myself to my feet. I turn to face him and bite my bottom lip. He is making me nervous now. "Have I done something...?" I ask and then cringe. What do I sound like? I lift my chin higher and fix a defiant look on my face, determined to change the tone of that sentence immediately. "Because if I have and you don't like it, go fuck yourself."

His look of surprise suddenly turns into a burst of laughter. "Feisty," he murmurs. "I like it."

I narrow my eyes and put my hands on my hips.

"Don't be so cold," he says, stepping closer. "Open up a bit. You are very frosty."

For a damn good reason. What is going on here?

He tenderly pulls me to him, and I sink into his embrace, feeling the strength from him and enjoying the feeling of being safe in his arms.

I look up and smile. He smiles back. I do something I'm not sure I'm ready for, but I know somehow that it's right. I press my lips against his.

He doesn't respond for a split second, but I figure that is just natural under the circumstances.

But then, he plunges his tongue into my mouth, his hand going into my wet hair to give me a kiss filled with such longing, I *know* something isn't right now. Declan's kisses are forceful and confident and completely sure. This is almost *needy*.

I pull back and frown, staring into his eyes, those deep blue eyes that have a slight spark there that I haven't seen before.

I jump back, my blood pounding in my ears when a familiar voice thunders from the doorway, "Cillian! Get your filthy fecking hands off her, you utter piece of shite."

Chapter Sixteen

Declan

Taking a deep breath and trying not to murder my twin brother where he stands, I enter Ruby's room slowly.

Cillian holds his hands up as Ruby gives him a ferocious glare that I'm glad I'm not on the receiving end of.

"What the fuck?" she growls, her old fire back in spades. "What the fuck is this? Some kind of twisted game?"

"Nope," Cillian says. "You asked for my help, so I helped. You never once asked if I was Declan."

She lets out a low rumble and picks up the hairbrush from the dresser. She throws it at Cillian with the force of...well, someone who has been stabbed in the gut four days ago. It bounces off his head and it's so comical, I let out a snort of amusement despite my anger at my brother.

"You," she hisses at me. "You never said you had a twin. I assumed he was you. Until I kissed him. Oh, then I knew, I *knew* something was off. His kisses suck!"

Her cheeks have gone bright red, which tells me she is

lying. Sure, different is probably accurate, not that I want to think about that, but suck? Yeah, nope. Not buying it.

"Really?" I drawl, giving Cillian a smug look anyway. Suddenly, I lose all of my anger at this and just find it funny. I have *no* idea why.

"Aren't you going to beat him to death?" Ruby fumes at me.

"If anyone is to blame here, it sounds like it was you," I retort.

She gapes at me. "You're taking *his* side?"

"By your own words, you said *you* kissed *him*," I reply.

"Fuck you," she snaps and stalks to the other side of the room where she catches herself and grabs her side in pain.

I rush straight for her, shoving Cillian out of my way. "Ruby," I say gently, taking her by the elbow and helping her sit. "Are you okay?"

She glares up at me with those pretty green eyes and then she does something that affects me in a sexual way, which is exactly what I was trying to avoid….she pouts at me.

"No," she says. "I'm not okay. He should've known that I didn't know, and *you* should've warned me."

"Well, I was kind of hoping you could tell the difference," I say lightly, trying not to make too big a deal out of the whole taking advantage angle. She doesn't seem to have latched onto that yet, so I'm skirting around it until she does. And if she does, *then* I will beat my brother to within an inch of his life.

The fire in her eyes is definitely the old Ruby. "You're putting this on me?" she shrieks.

"Sort of," I admit, sheepishly.

"Look, I didn't mean any harm," Cillian interjects into the simmering silence. "You asked for help, I helped and then you kissed me. I'm not in the business of turning away women who throw themselves at me."

She whips her head around to face him. "Throw myself at

you?" she growls. "You fucking wish. I thought you were *him*. I mean, hello? Have you looked in a mirror lately? No, I may not have asked if you were Declan but why would I when I didn't know he had a twin? Hmm? And another thing. I asked about Siobhan, so clearly I wasn't talking to you."

"Uhm," he says, giving me a raised eyebrow. "She doesn't know?"

"Siobhan and Cillian married shortly after we broke up. They're divorced now," I add hurriedly, "Just so you don't think you kissed a married man."

"So you make a habit of going after your brother's women, is that it?"

"Hardly," he scoffs. "Declan stole her from me in the first place…it's ancient history."

"Not. Quite," she clips out, seriously pissed off at me now.

I stroke her cheek with the back of my hand. "You're going to pull your stitches if you're not careful."

She rears back and then grimaces. "Oww," she cries.

"See," I mutter and then sigh. "I can break his nose if you really want me to."

She brightens considerably, forgetting about my transgression of many years ago, thank fuck. "You would?"

I nod.

"Hey," Cillian snaps. "I'm innocent over here."

"Innocent?" she scoffs. "Something tells me you were born a troublemaker."

I snort into my hand.

"Humph, well, then," Cillian says, acting all affronted. "I will see myself out. Ruby, it was nice to meet you regardless of you throwing me under the bus."

"Oh, please," she snaps. "You loved kissing me. It was probably the highlight of your year."

"That it was," he mutters with just enough longing in his

voice to warrant my attention. I wasn't overly concerned before now. Cillian is a strange one. Since his divorce, he has thrown himself into his work and hasn't been on a date in years. This was probably the first time he has kissed a woman in years. I can't say that I blame him for wanting to kiss her back. I *can* blame him for taking too much interest in her.

"Out," I snap and sit down on the bed next to Ruby. I eye her up speculatively. She has followed him with her eyes, and I can see a spark of interest in them.

"Are you sure you are okay?" I ask. "He shouldn't have pretended to be me."

She sighs. "No, you're both right. I should've known straight away. It was only when we kissed that I knew it wasn't you. Still, a heads up would've been good."

"I know. I was worried," I admit softly.

"What about? That I'd see you in him and want him too?"

I nod slowly. "Do you?"

"No," she says quickly. Too quickly. It doesn't take an eye trained to pick up every single movement and facial expression to know that given half the chance, she'd kiss him again. I don't know how I feel about that. The other men are hers. They always were and always will be. Cillian, though? He is someone she knows through me and that doesn't sit right with me, somehow. Twin or not. Brother or not. I would not feel good enough if she decided to pursue him.

Not that I think she would right now anyway. So I'm probably being paranoid.

She wraps her arms around me, and I kiss the top of her head, then I tilt her chin up and press my lips against hers. She opens up and I sweep my tongue briefly over hers and then I pull back. "That's what you wanted, wasn't it?"

She nods. "I'm nowhere near even close to being ready for anything else, but a kiss, I can do," she murmurs. Then her face crumples as it hits her what just happened. *Now*, I'm ready to kill for her regardless of who it is. "He came into my room, and I thought he was you," she whispers. "I was defenseless."

"Hey," I say, holding her tightly. "Cillian is a dick, but he would *never* hurt you. I know you don't know that, but I do, and I need you to trust me. Can you do that? Can you accept that you were in no danger?"

She gives a little shrug, picking at the towel wrapped around her body. I lean over and pull the coverlet over her, giving her some protection against the vulnerability she is feeling. "Still want me to kick his head in?" I ask.

Her laugh is a snuffly one, but she shakes her head. "Don't suppose your mom would appreciate me very much if I got in the middle of you two."

"Oh, she'd be on your side," I inform her truthfully. "Mam is very much a woman's woman. She would lay down her life if it meant saving another. It's her way of dealing with what happened to her."

"Your dad?" she asks carefully.

I nod and brush it aside. I *don't* want to talk about it.

"I'm here to talk to, you know," she says.

She's the sweetest thing. Worried about me when she is going through her own trauma. "I know."

"I don't want..." she huffs out a breath and looks away.

"Don't want what?" I press, knowing what she's going to say anyway.

"I don't want Scarlet having that part of you. You are *mine* in every way."

"I am," I reply, my cold heart filling with warmth at her words. "And you are mine. You are my priority now. I need you to heal and claim back your power and strength before I will ever allow myself to come first."

"Too sweet," she murmurs. "Just for the record, you kiss way better than Cillian," she adds with a smile.

"I know," I reply, making her laugh and it lights up the darkness, just a tiny bit.

Chapter Seventeen

Ruby

Two Weeks Later

I replace the cap and place the stick on the countertop. I set the timer on my phone and then gently close the lid of the toilet to sit on it, bringing my knees up to rest my chin on. It tugs on my scar, but I'm healing up nicely and can mobilize much faster and with more ease than before. Thank fuck. If I had to walk up and down stairs one at a time for the rest of my life, I would go insane.

I lick my lips and wait.

Three weeks have passed since…that day. I was due my period two days ago. I don't know if it's the stress, the trauma or the dreaded 'p' word that has caused me to be late. I'm not one to sit around waiting either. It has taken me these two days to get away from Declan for long enough to walk to the pharmacy in the small village to buy a pregnancy test.

I'll admit that as I wait for the three minutes to be up, I'm scared. It is both the fact that I *could* be pregnant, but also the fact that it might not belong to one of the men that I care about. We all know condoms and the pill aren't a hundred percent protection, even together. What if it broke? What if he had super-sperm that shot through? What if my pill failed for some reason…? What if…?

Just, what if it's *his*?

I couldn't bear it.

I know I don't want kids. I had already made that decision years ago after I had a scare big enough to make me start looking at bassinets to buy. Derek was sweet, said he'd marry me and all that, but it wasn't what I wanted. I considered having an abortion, but that just bordered on repulsive to me, so I stopped thinking about it as an option at the time. I was only twenty-two years old, and he was my first lover after the rape. Freshly moved from the States and trying to make my name over here with Derek's help, I got involved with him when I knew I shouldn't have. Half of me suspects he tried to get me pregnant on purpose. He was always talking about having a family, a *legacy*, I think he tried to have that with me because I was too doe-eyed and naïve to say no. I don't hate him for it, maybe if it had turned out to be true, I would feel differently, but the false positive was proven when I finally got my period three weeks later. Or maybe I had a miscarriage. Who knows? Now, if I'm pregnant, there will be no way to know whose it is. I can't take the chance. I will *have* to get an abortion.

I bite my lip and then stand up as the scar starts to protest too much. I pace up and down and then the three minutes are up.

With sweaty palms and a pounding heart, I pick up the pregnancy test and glare at it.

Inhaling deeply, I meet my eyes in the mirror and shove it

in the back pocket of my jeans as there is a soft knock on the bathroom door.

"Ruby?"

I plaster a smile on my face and open the door. "Hey," I say to Declan.

"Everything okay?"

"You don't need to hover, I'm fine," I reply.

"Can we talk?" he asks, looking nervous.

I frown and let him lead me into my bedroom "What's up?" I ask.

He sits on the bed and takes a deep breath. I move around to the other side and quietly open the nightstand drawer, slipping the pregnancy test into it and closing it again.

"How do you feel about me still working?" he asks.

"What do you mean?" I ask back, going over to sit next to him.

"I mean, me going to work," he replies exasperated.

"I know that," I snap. "I mean, why are you asking me?"

"I don't want to leave you, but a job has come up. It's in Belfast, not that far away, I just…I don't want to leave you."

"I'm fine," I say again and realize that maybe I need to shake up my crappy response before he suspects something *isn't* fine. "I get that you need to work. I'm okay here, I promise."

"Are you sure?" he asks, his brow creasing.

I nod.

"Cillian will look out for you."

My heart skips a beat. I haven't seen his twin since the day we kissed. I assumed Declan had warned him to stay away, but this says the opposite. "Oh?" I ask, my voice a small squeak.

"He is in the right industry to look out for you. He will protect you and our mam."

I narrow my eyes and then it strikes me. He is worried about leaving *me* here with his mom. Me the troublemaker.

"I can go back to England with the other men," I say stiffly. Not insulted, per se. Just a bit hurt because how could I not be. But I understand his hesitation. I would be the same with my mom.

"No!" he says instantly. "No, I want you to stay. I just need to know that you and Mam will be safe. It's okay, I won't go. It's fine."

Well, 'fine' crunched it all down for me. I used fine and it wasn't, so I don't believe him one bit.

"Declan, look. If Cillian is here to watch out for us, then you can go. What does he do anyway?" I ask casually, suddenly desperate to know.

Declan's eyes meet mine with reluctance. "He is part of the Irish mafia," he states.

"Ooh," I say, trying to feign disinterest but WHOA!

It all makes sense now why he barely talks about his twin. He knew we would have so much in common and with Cillian looking exactly like him, he got insecure. It's so super sweet, I smile and run my hand through his dark hair.

"See, I knew that would pique your interest! It's why I didn't tell you!" he exclaims.

"Declan, don't be ridiculous. You are the man I want to be with. Yes, I'm intrigued, but so what? He lives here and I live over there and I'm with you and the other men. Plus, the whole…you know…"

He sighs. "Yeah, I know. Sorry for being a paranoid arsehole. Old habit."

I kiss him briefly, still a little gun-shy. Not because I think it might be Cillian lurking pretending to be Declan, but because I don't want to give him, any of them, the false hope that things are getting back to normal.

They aren't.

Not by a long shot, and that both worries and scares me.

"Go and do your job. Your mom and I will be perfectly safe here. You know I won't let anything happen to her."

"If anyone does...come here...you are in no way to confront them, Ruby. Leave it to Cillian and his men. They'll be watching the house twenty-four seven. If anyone slips through the net, please, please promise me that you will run or hide or something."

"I don't know if you know me, but running and hiding is not really my style. Now fighting and stabbing, that's my thing."

He snorts. "Yes, I'm aware and that's what scares me the most about leaving you. You have no fear and will dive in headfirst."

"I have fear," I say lightly.

"No," he shakes his head. "You work on instinct and it's on point. Look at what you managed to do three weeks ago," he adds quietly. "I don't know of anyone who could've done what you did."

I bite my tongue, hurting myself.

I try not to think about that day. I know he wants to talk about it. They all do. They have all tried over the last two weeks, but I don't want to. I just want to forget.

"If I promise not to dive in headfirst, will you go? I don't want you to stop working because of me. I know you need that to deal with your demons."

He nods slowly. "When I get back, we'll talk. I'll tell you all about it."

I smile. "I'd like that."

"On one condition," he adds sternly.

"Hm?"

"You have to talk too."

"Sure," I lie.

He knows it, I know it. But fuck it.

He presses his lips together, not pushing me and he stands

up. "I've been putting this off for weeks. If I'm going, I need to go today."

I stand too. "Go. I'll miss you, and I'll be a good girl while you're gone."

"I'm counting on it," he says and tilts my chin up before he plants a light kiss on my lips. I deepen it, giving him what he needs. He accepts it, but doesn't take it further. He allows me to break it off and step back.

"I love you, Ruby," he murmurs. "I'll be back soon."

I nod and watch him go.

As soon as he closes the door behind him, I practically fly across the bed in my haste to yank the nightstand drawer open to double-check that I saw what I saw before.

Negative.

I breathe a sigh of relief and flop back to the bed, grateful that whatever deity is out there, didn't choose this moment to fuck with me.

I can keep moving forwards. One step at a time.

Chapter Eighteen

Ruby

About an hour later, I head downstairs. Declan has left and in his place is Cillian, sitting in an armchair with a cup of coffee.

"How?" I ask with narrowed eyes.

"How what?" he asks warily. "Hang on, before we go any further...I'm..."

"Cillian," I interrupt. "I know. I can tell you apart. *Now*."

He smirks. "Good to know. How what?"

"How did you get a cup of coffee? Your mom only makes me tea."

"You need to know where it's kept," he replies with a laugh. "Here."

He stands up and hands it to me. I take it and savor the small sip. "God, it's been too long. I think I have withdrawals."

"I could take you for a real cup," he says casually.

"Does that fall under the category of protection?" I ask, handing him the cup back.

"From yourself? Sure."

"Smart-ass," I grumble, but he's not wrong. I would murder for some caffeine and that's not a threat to be taken lightly. "Fine. Let me get changed."

"You look fine," he says. "Besides. I want to show you something."

"Oh?" I ask, intrigued. "What's that then?"

"Well, Declan tells me you have barely left the house since you got here. He also told me what you really do, and I want to show you what *I* do."

"He already told me," I say, my mouth going dry.

"I know, but can I show you?"

I nod slowly. I really do want to get out of here. I've been cooped up for too long. Even though I haven't actually wanted to go anywhere. The trip out to the pharmacy was out of necessity, and the one trip to the cottage that the guys are staying in, was a disaster a week ago. I panicked, they flapped, and then Declan brought me home. Think I was gone twenty minutes, tops.

"Okay," I say decisively. "Give me a minute."

He nods and sits back down.

I take the stairs steadily, hoping that I'm making the right decision and won't end up making a fool of myself.

I swap my slippers for some sneakers and grab my coat. I wish I had my knives, but I had to leave them behind due to the flight over. I bite my lip and change my mind about going, but then I glance out of the window. It's sunny and blue skies, and even though it's freezing, it will do my head good to get out of here.

Heading back down the stairs, I see Cillian waiting for me by the door. I take a deep breath and smile.

"I'm ready," I say.

He nods and opens the door for me. I hesitate, and he sees it. He takes a step forward and out the door, holding his hand out for me to follow.

"Thanks," I mutter and take it.

It's like an electric shock. I gasp and try to pull my hand back, but he grips my fingers tightly, leading me towards his flashy white Ferrari parked in the driveway.

"Nice," I murmur and slip inside when he opens the passenger door for me.

I make myself comfortable in the bucket seat, my hands fisted on my lap in nervousness. Declan said that Cillian would never hurt me. I'm not in any danger. I'm safe.

I keep telling myself this when he sets off, and soon we are headed into the city, while he keeps up a one-sided conversation about his business.

It helps me relax and after a wildly exaggerated story, I'm sure, I laugh and become completely at ease with him.

"You don't believe me?" he asks with a laugh.

"What? That you chopped his dick off and ate it like a sausage?" I snort. "Wasn't that an episode of Game of Thrones?"

He lets out a loud guffaw as he pulls up behind a warehouse on the outskirts of the city. "Ah, you got me," he concedes, "But it made you laugh."

He grins at me, and I return it. "Yes, it did. It feels like a million years since I laughed so hard."

He climbs out of the car and rushes around to open up my side, even though I was part way through doing it myself.

"Mi'lady," he says with a bow.

"Fuck off," I retort, but take his arm anyway.

After unlocking the back door with a keycard *and* a code, he opens it and goes through, stepping aside to let me in. I'm faced with another door, this one made from reinforced steel with a biometric scanner connected to it.

Cillian closes the first door and then leans in to open the second door by placing his eye to the scanner.

It clicks open, and a thrill goes down my spine. He ushers me inside and closes the door with a loud thunk.

"Wow," I comment, taking in the operation before my eyes. "Just like this?"

He nods. "The *Garda* don't swing by unannounced," he says, tapping his nose.

I shudder and push crooked cops as far from my mind as I can. I clear my throat. "So this is your whole counterfeit operation?"

"Yep. Split into currency. Dollars on the far side, Pounds in the middle and Euros here in front of us."

"Impressive," I murmur. The printing machines are loud and continuous, with workers scurrying back and forth between the presses and the lines to dry it all out. There's a chopping section and another one bagging it all up. It's a well-oiled machine. "This all yours?" I ask.

"I have my cut," he says, but adds nothing else.

That confirms to me that he has a boss. I wonder who that is, but don't ask.

He leads me towards an office at the back and indicates I should sit in one of the chairs opposite his desk. "I'll just be a minute and then we can head out for that coffee," he says, seeming distracted by a file on his desk. He scans through it, his face going darker.

The minutes tick by. I think he has forgotten I'm here.

I'm about to speak up when there is a solid knock on the door and Cillian calls out, "Yeah?"

When the door opens, I shrink back in my chair.

An enormous man, with chest tattoos that are visible over the top of his extremely well-fitted, white t-shirt strides in, his eyes zooming straight to me.

I gulp.

They are dark, almost black. His hair is the same color as soot, and it matches his soul. *If* he has one. I've done business with some shady characters in the past, hell, I *am* one of them, but Jesus fucking Christ. This guy is completely devoid of anything light. He has the look of a true psychopath, and I feel fear shoot through me. My fingers reach for my knife, but it's not there. I start to panic slightly. My breathing becomes shallow and my eyes blur. He interrupts my attack, by taking a step closer.

"Who are you?" he growls, his Irish accent thick and deep.

"Never mind her, Tadgh," Cillian barks out, barely looking up from the file. "She belongs to Declan."

I turn my head to Cillian, my mouth dropping open in disdain. *Belong*? Who the fuck does he think he's talking about?

I'm about to stand up, grab him by the collar and yank him over his desk while I educate him on the finer aspects of being an independent woman, when his eyes meet mine and in their blue depths, there is a warning for me to shut the hell up and stay still. I shut my mouth, but I can't help looking back over at Tadgh. His dead black eyes hold my gaze for a second before he drops it in a very clear sign of submission.

Well, fuck.

What is that about?

"You read that file?" Tadgh asks Cillian, his rough and ready attitude dimmed slightly now.

"Yeah," Cillian replies and slams it shut. "You know what to do?"

Tadgh nods and then backs out of the office, slamming the door behind him.

I raise my eyebrow at Cillian. "*Belong* to Declan," I snap, unable to help myself now that the threat is gone.

Cillian waves his hand dismissively. "Don't get your knickers in a twist. There are very few people who intimidate Tadgh. Declan is one of them. In case you hadn't noticed just by looking at him, he is a bit of a sociopath."

That makes my blood run cooler. Somehow that scares me more if it's an accurate assessment. Boomer was a complete psychopath. He had absolutely no conscience, no moral compass, no consideration of right or wrong. Tadgh is the opposite of that. He knows, he just doesn't care and rationalizes his behavior. The tendency to be impulsive and hot-headed is what makes sociopaths unpredictable, and therefore more dangerous in my book. Although the opposite is usually true, case and point, Boomer, one could point out that *I* am a bit of a sociopath myself. That's what makes it scarier. I *know* what I'm capable of.

"Knife," I blurt out. "Do you have one?"

Cillian's concerned eyes hood slightly, but he reaches down into a drawer and pulls out the most beautiful black, double-bladed knife and hands it to me, hilt first.

As soon as it hits my hand, I feel better. I relax and stick the tip of my finger on the point of one of the blades and twirl it around. "Pretty," I murmur.

"I'll need that back before you leave the country," he says.

"Mean something to you?" I ask.

"You could say that," he replies cagily.

I huff out a breath and stand up. I start to pace. "We're a lot alike," I say.

"I know," he says.

"Declan knows too."

"He does."

"I like the way you look at me."

"Oh?" he croaks out, standing suddenly.

"You don't look at me like I'm a fragile china doll that has been physically and mentally abused."

"Why would I?" he asks carefully.

"He didn't tell you?"

Cillian shakes his head slowly.

"Good. That's good. I'm sick of being the victim! I'm sick

to death of being scared, and I'm sick of constantly thinking about being sexually assaulted and stabbed in the gut while I was helpless!" I roar and with all the pent-up anger and frustration coursing through me, I throw the knife at the wall next to where Cillian is standing. There's that hotheadedness and impulsiveness, I was talking about.

Unpredictable.

The blade buries deep into the plasterboard and vibrates as we both look at it.

"I need to get out of here," I shriek and aim for the door, almost hoping I run into Tadgh so I can show him exactly what I'm made of. Right now, I would rip him to shreds with my bare hands. There is fire in my veins, blood roaring in my ears. I'm hot and sweaty and the feeling of the walls closing in is making it hard to breathe.

I wasn't ready.

I should've stayed back at Mary's where I was safe, and away from people.

I burst through the reinforced steel door, easily opened from this side and then yank the next door open, stumbling through, bouncing off the doorjamb and hurting my arm.

I gulp in a deep breath and the open space, the fresh air, has the opposite effect on me. I panic more.

I lunge for the car door, noticing earlier that Cillian didn't bother to lock it down this back alley. I fall into the passenger seat and slam the door.

I close my eyes and take a steady breath. Then another.

This feeling has to end. I can't stand it. I need a release. I need...

"Fuuuuck," I moan when I know exactly what I need.

I slip my hand into the waistband of my sweats and inch my fingers towards my pussy. I freeze, but then curse myself for being an idiot. These are *my* fingers, godammit. If I don't do this, if I don't bring myself to an orgasm, I feel like my head is going to explode. I need to do this to release the tension but also to release the fear. I can't bear it any longer.

I shove my hand into my panties and finger my clit roughly.

I scrunch my eyes up even more, pushing the image of Smith out of my head. "You don't belong in here," I moan.

With my breathing ragged, I slow down and start to rotate my middle finger over my clit. I'm as dry as the desert, but I don't care. I *need* to do this. I don't care if my orgasm is like a puff of pleasure. It's a start to get over this fear.

I moan, hurting myself as I dry up even more, but I power on. Stopping now is defeat, and my fragile psyche can't take that right now.

"Ruby."

My eyes fly open at the sound of Cillian's voice on the outside of the car window.

I gasp as my clit twitches, and I feel a puddle form at my entrance.

"Shit," I pant.

Cillian opens the car door and then freezes when he sees me with my hand down my pants.

"Oh, feck," he groans and turns away.

"No!" I shout at him. "Look at me!"

"Ruby...I..."

"Please, look at me," I beg him, rubbing my slippery clit with more vigor.

I have my right hand occupied, but my left one is ready to stop him if he touches me. I just want him to watch. It has spiked my arousal, which I thought was dead.

Cillian crouches down and drops his eyes to my hand moving inside my sweats. He doesn't say a word. He just watches me as I asked.

I feel my clit twitch again and then the orgasm washes

over, making me buck in the car seat as I let out a soft cry of relief.

I did it.

I pant and remove my hand, clenching it into a fist.

"Thank you," I murmur, feeling embarrassed but elated.

"No, thank *you*," he says with a smirk, and places the beautiful black knife on my lap. I snatch it up quickly.

I giggle, but then sober up. "Thank you for not trying to touch me."

His serious eyes meet mine. "I know survivors of sexual assault, Ruby. You don't ever have to fear me. I am here to help you in any way that I can. But I won't touch you. I will respect your boundaries and those of your men. Declan has told me a lot about you, and I feel like you wouldn't want me to do something without their consent. Get it, and then we'll talk more."

"What makes you think I want to talk?" I croak.

"We are two sides of the same coin, Ruby. If you get consent from your men to explore whatever this is that we have, and I *know* you feel it too, then we'll talk."

I bite the inside of my lip and nod, not able to say a word because he's right. I do need to seek consent, but first there is something else I need and without Declan here to give it to me, Layton is going to have to step up.

Chapter Nineteen

Layton

I'm trying not to think about being away from Ruby anymore. It's doing my head in, and I can't stand the thought of anything bad happening to her because I'm not there to protect her. I have to put my faith in Declan and trust that we will be returning to Manchester soon. I look up from where I was hovering at the window that overlooks the back garden of this 3-bedroom cottage not far from Declan's mum's place, when there is a banging on the door.

"What the fuck?" David asks, leaping up from the armchair where he was comfy with his laptop.

I stride over and open it, ready to growl at the person on the other side when Ruby falls forward, her fist in the air, having been about to bang again.

I catch her by her elbow and steady her, but then let her go. "Ruby?"

"Layton," she pants. "I need you."

"What's happened?" I ask, my blood running cold.

She barges past me, which is not an easy task, leaving me to stare at the white Ferrari in the driveway with Declan leaning up against it.

"Thought you were gone," I snarl.

"Cillian," he says. "Not Declan, just to get that out there straight away."

"Humph," I mutter. I've heard about this twin. I need to keep my eye on him.

"Ruby asked me to bring her here. Take care of her," he says and straightens up, giving me a shrewd look before he climbs back into the car and fires off.

I shut the door and turn to face Ruby. She is beyond agitated. She is pacing and fretful and something isn't right.

"What is it?" I ask gently.

"I did something," she says. "Something bad!"

"Whatever it is, we can talk about it," I say quietly, calmly because she is losing it. I don't approach her, knowing it will only send her even more over the edge, so I stay where I am. Unfortunately, that has an undesirable effect.

She drops to her hands and knees and crawls towards me. "Layton, please. Without Declan here, I need you to do this for me."

My stomach twists.

I can't bear to see her prostrate herself in front of me. Not now. Not like this. How the fuck does Declan handle this?

I crouch down so that I'm at her level and ask, "Do what?"

"Absolve me," she sobs. "I did something bad to you. To all of you. It was wrong, but I needed to do it."

I look up as Ramsey has come closer. David is still standing by the armchair, clutching his laptop like a deer in headlights.

"What did you do?" I ask, my mouth going dry. This has something to do with Cillian, I'm sure of it.

"Please, let me confess."

"Okay," I say reassuringly. Her eyes have gone wild, and

I'm worried about her having a breakdown. I take her wrist and stand up, hauling her up with me. "Okay." I let go of her and hold my hands up slightly so she can see I'm not intent on restraining her.

"Tell me what you did," I murmur. There is no chance in hell I'm going to whip her, even if she begs me. I'm not hurting her for anything. It's not my place. I hate that Declan had to do that the other week. It sickens me, but I saw how much she needed it. It was easy to let him deal with it. He knows what he's doing in that area. They have their roles set. This makes me uneasy because it isn't in a setting that I'm used to. If this were sexual, I could handle it without a single hesitation, but this is as far from that as possible.

"Take your belt off," she says and turns around, stripping her coat off.

David's gasp gets me to move forward from the freezing stillness that had fallen over me.

"No," I say steadily. "Tell me what you did first and then I will punish you if I see fit."

What the fuck else can I say? Damn you Declan for leaving.

Her shoulders slump and she bows her head. "I was with Cillian earlier," she starts and my heart stops beating. If she tells me that he touched her in any way, I will go back out there, track him down and beat him to a pulp before I rip his heart out with my bare hands.

"I had a panic attack, but then I got pissed. Really pissed about all of this. I hate being this way. So scared, so vulnerable. I needed to do *something* to push past it. I needed to take back control of my own body."

"Oh?" David croaks out.

I shoot him a glare to shut the hell up. The last thing we want is to judge her.

She nods. "I started to masturbate. It was awful. I was so alone and terrified of what I was doing, but I *needed* it."

"You were...alone?" I ask carefully.

She nods. "But then Cillian came to find me, and it lit a spark deep inside me. I *felt* something. I was aroused. I wanted him to watch. He didn't want to, he wanted to leave, but I begged him to stay. He did. He watched me come and I liked it. I'm so sorry." She falls to her knees again.

"Did he touch you," I rasp.

"No. He didn't. He was perfect. He knows what I need, and he knows that without your consent, with *my* consent, he won't do anything. He wants to. We both do. There's something there...Declan knows. It's why he was so afraid to tell me about him."

"You want him?" I feel like my life is draining away.

"Not in that sense," she whispers. "I can't. Not yet. But..."

Relief floods me. She didn't go to him for something that she thought we couldn't give her. She just needed him to be there to make her feel secure, so she could push past the crippling fear she was feeling. I can live with that. It remains to be seen if I, or any of us, can accept him in her life as one of us. I wonder what Declan has to say about that.

"You did nothing wrong, sweetheart," I tell her after a beat. "You did what you needed to do to take control. None of us blame you for that."

"I blame myself," she mutters.

"Well, don't," I say and go to her. I stroke her hair and she lets me.

"Please forgive me."

"There is nothing to forgive," I whisper.

"Please," she says, looking up at me with tears running down her cheeks.

I sigh and make a decision. There is only one thing I can think of right now how to handle this. I take her hand and lead her up the stairs to the master bedroom. Ramsey and David follow close behind.

I can sense their unasked questions, their fear at what I'm going to do, but they needn't worry. It's not something that will break her. She has a choice to make.

I stop at the big, walk-in wardrobe with the sliding door and open it.

"Get in," I say. "If you really feel like you need absolution for what you did, get in the wardrobe and stay there until I come back for you."

You could hear a pin drop in the silence that follows.

She takes a step forward, pulling out of my grasp and enters the wardrobe. She sits on the floor, her back against the wall, her legs stretched out.

Her eyes find mine and I nod. I slide the door closed, leaving her in the dark, enclosed space, hating myself for what I'm doing but I have no choice. Declan isn't here to decide what to do with her and this is the best I've got that doesn't require anything physical. If she didn't want to do it, she didn't have to. I gave her a choice and she made it.

I brush past David and Ramsey and walk slowly down the stairs. There is a phone call I have to make, and I need to do it now.

Pulling my phone out of my back pocket, I dial quickly as Ramsey and David thunder back down the stairs.

"You can't leave her in there," David exclaims as Declan answers the video call.

"What is it?" he asks immediately.

I fill him in, and he nods grimly. "I see," he says.

"And?" Ransey asks. "What do you make of all this?"

"If she wants him, we can't stop her," he says, even though his face pretty much looks like he wants to stop her.

"That's your verdict?" I ask.

He nods. "I knew this was coming. I saw them kiss. It

was…" He sighs. "I knew it was coming. I've made peace with it."

"Really?" David asks. "Because you look like you're about to throw up."

I stifle my snicker. Always count on David to bring his sunshine to a dark situation.

"I agree," I say, knowing it is the only thing we can do. "We have to give her our consent to pursue their relationship."

"I don't want to," David sulks.

"You have to," Declan says. "She won't be happy if she doesn't. It's not for us to decide if she is unhappy for the rest of her life. She needs to try. If it fails, then at least she knows."

"Yeah," Ramsey says. "We don't have a choice."

"So, it's decided," I state and get a murmur of agreement.

"Gotta go," Declan says and hangs up quickly.

"How long will you leave her in there?" David asks, changing his tune now and figuring she needs a time out.

"Half an hour, tops. If she wants to leave, she knows she can."

He nods and I turn from them to head into the kitchen. If anytime called for a cup of hot chocolate, now is that time. I have to wrap my head around learning to share her with another man, one who looks exactly like Declan.

Weird doesn't even cover this situation, but Declan is right.

It's not up to us to hold her back if she decides she wants Cillian to join us. We have to accept her choices and move on with it.

Chapter Twenty

David

Fifteen minutes have passed since Layton told Ruby to go into the wardrobe. I know there's a joke about Narnia in there somewhere, but I can't summon up the amusement. I hover at the bottom of the stairs, but then make the decision and start going up. I feel Layton's eyes on my back, but sod it. I'm just as much a part of this as he is.

Stopping at the wardrobe, I hear her say, "David."

"How did you know it was me?" I ask with a smile.

"Layton and Ramsey aren't as light-footed as you," she says with a snort.

I chuckle and slide the door open. "Do you want to come out?"

"Nope."

"Can I come in?"

"Yup."

I sink to the floor and crawl into the wardrobe with her.

She is lying down now on her side, her hands under her head. I stick my feet at the opposite end to hers and lie down facing her.

"Are you okay in here?"

"Yes," she says. "It's quite peaceful."

"Okay, good," I say with relief. I was dreading it being the opposite, especially if she had a panic attack.

"Do you forgive me?" she asks.

"There's nothing to forgive," I say lightly.

"There is. That's why I'm in the closet."

I can't help the burst of laughter. "Sorry, but come on. You're in here with me."

She giggles. She seems fine. "I can think of a few more jokes about being in here."

"Narnia?" I ask.

"Yes!" she cries and snorts with laughter but then she goes serious again. "Do you forgive me?"

"Rubes…" I sigh in exasperation.

"David, look. I know you don't get this whole absolution thing. And I don't expect you to understand it. When I come out of here, Layton and Declan and even Ramsey will have seen it as penance. I'm not sure you do. And that's fine."

"Well, you have me there," I mutter. "I don't fully understand it. I'm trying to and I will eventually wrap my head around it. So if you need to hear the words from me, then yes, I forgive you."

"Thank you," she whispers, almost breaking my heart.

We sit in silence for a while.

"I think I want to go home," she says quietly.

"Are you ready for that?" I ask carefully.

"I think so."

"What about Cillian?"

I hear her shrug her shoulders. "Don't know. We need to talk."

"You will come back from this, Ruby," I venture after a beat. "Stronger than ever."

"I know."

"I hope you do, because I believe it. I've always believed in you, since the day I first met you at Derek's office. He loved you so much," I add quietly. "He was in awe of you. He said you were a dark goddess. I didn't get what he meant at the time, but I do now. I was so jealous of him. Working for him started to become a massive pain in the arse because all he would do is gush about you. Before he died, he knew it was coming."

"Oh?" she croaks out.

"Yeah, he made sure that I promised to go and work for you. He said he would make sure you asked because you needed me. You needed me to bring a bit of light to your world. He knew you had a glowing future ahead of you, and he wanted me there so you would always have someone you could trust. A light in your darkness that would guide you home."

She doesn't say anything. I know she still gets a bit upset over Derek's death. He was her mentor. He wanted so much more than she was prepared to give, but it didn't stop him from making sure she was set up with the keys to his kingdom before he was taken out.

"He said all that?" she whispers.

"He did."

"You *are* my light, David. You always have been, I just didn't really see it before in all the murk."

My heart pounds in my chest when she feels for my fingers and grips them tightly.

"Don't ever stop being that for me. I think I would truly fall if you did."

I shuffle over to kiss her forehead. "You don't have to

worry about that. I love you, Ruby and that will never change."

"I mean, don't ever lose your light. This world is…well, you know. I don't need to spell it out for you. I'm going back to it after this. I can't say for sure something like this will never happen again. Is it going to stop me? Fuck, no. I won't let it beat me, or scare me into giving up everything I've worked for. But it chips away at your soul. I'm scared that you will become like me."

"I can't promise what the future brings, Rubes," I say lightly. "But I do know that I will always be what you need me to be. Even if the light fades, it will always shine only for you."

"Move in with me," she blurts out.

I blink in the darkness. "What?" I ask, sure I didn't hear that right.

"When we get back home, move into my house. I don't mean romantically, not yet anyway, but I need to keep you close. All of you."

"Have you asked the others yet?" I ask, hoping that I'm the first one. It's silly, but it's a valid reaction in my case. I don't feel inferior to the other men, exactly, but they are all big, badasses and I'm…just me.

"Not yet. I only just thought of it. We need to stick together. I need you, all of you, close by."

"Then consider it done," I reply.

"Thanks," she mutters.

"You ready to get out of this cupboard?"

"Yes," she says and sits up.

I stand and help her up.

"Before we go out there. I'm glad that you managed to find a way to beat the fear. I'm glad Cillian was there for you. You have my blessing if you want to give it a go with him."

I slide the door open in time to see her smile. "Thank you. I really needed to hear that from you, especially."

"Anytime," I reply, but then frown. "Well, no, not anytime. Last time, 'kay?"

Her smile widens and she nods. "Promise."

With her looking a hundred times better than she did when she arrived here, holding hands, we head down the stairs, and for the first time since this happened to her, I actually feel like this won't destroy us and we might make it through this in one piece.

Chapter Twenty-One

Ramsey

I don't know what to think. In fact, the more I think, the more confused I get. It isn't about another guy joining us in this relationship, it's the fact that it's Declan's twin. How weird is that going to be? I have never met this guy but how much does he look like Declan? Enough to fool Ruby and that worries me. I don't want her to have to wonder which one is which every time she's with them. It's stress she doesn't need.

I look up from my simmering silence when I hear her and David coming down the stairs. She is smiling and seems happy. That's a good sign, right?

"Hey," she says shyly.

"You okay, sweetheart?" Layton growls as I go to her and kiss the top of her head.

"Yeah, I'm good. Honestly, I haven't felt this good in a while. David tells me that you had a discussion about Cillian."

I nod.

"And you're all okay with whatever is going on?" she presses.

"What *is* going on?" I blurt out.

"Not sure yet," she replies candidly. "He gets me and it's nice to have someone in the same business as me, even if it's here."

"About that..." Layton starts, but she shakes her head.

"I don't know," she interrupts. "I really don't know."

We all turn to look at Layton when his phone rings and we see it's Declan on a video call.

"Princess," he growls. "Did Layton take good care of you?"

She nods. "He did buuut, he's too soft. I need you back here."

Layton splutters as I stifle a laugh. I don't think anyone could accuse Layton of being soft. He's one of the hardest men I know. But with her, he's different.

Declan smiles at her. "Not long now."

"When you come back, I want to go home," she says. "I'm ready."

"Are you sure?" I ask with a frown.

She nods. "Yeah. It's time."

"If you are absolutely sure, we can do that," Declan says. "But you're welcome to stay with me mam for as long as you like."

"She's the best, honestly, but I need to get back. Hiding out here is adding to my anxiety."

"Okay," he says. "Give me two days and then I'll be back."

He hangs up and she looks up at me, "Drive me home? I want to talk to you about something."

I blink, surprised, but say, "Sure." I take the keys that Layton holds out and wait as she says her goodbyes.

Once we are in the Range Rover and have set off in the

general direction of Declan's mum's house, Ruby says, "I need you to move in with me."

"Uhm," I stammer, wondering where this is coming from. Trauma? Fear?

"I know how it sounds," she says with a soft laugh, "but I'm not asking you to move into my bedroom. Just my house. With David and Declan and hopefully, also Layton. I haven't asked him yet."

"So I'm third on the list?" I ask with a smirk. I'm not insulted, just surprised.

"No," she says, shaking her head. "Declan is already living there in the overnight room, and I just asked David before. It came out before I meant it to, but once it was out there, I needed to make sure you and Layton were in the loop."

"So, it's for protection?" I ask, scrunching up my nose.

"Yes, yours and mine," she replies lightly.

"Safety in numbers, like?"

"Something like that," she agrees with a smile.

"If you think you, or we, will be in danger when we get home, shouldn't we stay here for a bit longer?" I ask a reasonable question.

"I don't think we will be in any particular danger, no more so than usual. Jake is dead, and whoever has slipped into his place will be too busy trying to play catch up to bother about me. This is more general than that. We caused a lot of trouble before we left. I think it's best if we stick together."

"Okay," I say. "I'm in. As long as I don't have to share a room with Layton."

"You will have your own room. Why, what's wrong with sharing with Layton?"

"Nothing if you can sleep properly, which I don't. He is a terrible insomniac. Worse than me. What little sleep I get, I want to be asleep."

"Hmm, why is that?" she asks out of the blue.

It disarms me.

Wily creature. She's been waiting for the chance.

"If you really want to know, my mum used to get pissed up and high, and her friends would come over. They'd party all night long and then when it came to bedtime...let's just say any bed would do."

I stare grimly in front of me, shuddering from the memories of those old skanks climbing in bed with me.

"Oh, baby," she murmurs, placing her hand on my thigh. It's the first time she has initiated contact with me since that day, and it blows all the shit away. I smile at her before turning back to the road.

"It's fine," I lie, shrugging. "It just made me a wary sleeper and that grew into barely sleeping at all."

"Yeah, I can imagine," she murmurs. "Uhm, I think that was our turning..." she adds, looking back at the road we've just driven past.

"You sure?" I ask with a frown. "I thought it was the next one."

"Oh, maybe..." she says.

"Layton always drives," I complain. "I actually don't have a fucking clue where I'm going."

"Me either," she says with a laugh.

"Check the Satnav," I instruct her. "Maybe it can tell us where we've been."

"Good idea," she says and leans forward, taking her hand off my leg to fiddle with the built-in GPS system.

"Oh, here," she says after a minute. "That's it. Bluebell Terrace." She punches some buttons and soon we are rerouted and on our way for real.

Ten minutes later, we pull up outside the huge home Mrs. Gannon lives in and I cut the engine. I turn to her and smile, brushing her dark hair away from her face.

"Safe and sound," I murmur.

"Thanks," she says and leans forward to press her lips to mine.

I panic.

I don't know if I should push her away, kiss her back or just let her kiss me.

In the end, she thrusts her tongue into my mouth and my body takes over. I twist my tongue around hers and enjoy the first kiss I've had with her in weeks.

She ends the kiss by biting my bottom lip and tugging it gently, making my dick go so hard, I want to cry. I hope she hasn't noticed. I don't want to scare her or do anything to upset her. I shift awkwardly in my seat and clear my throat. She gives me a knowing smile and then climbs out of the car.

I start to get out, but she stops me with a mumbled, "Nuh-uh."

"The curtains are twitching," she says, trying to suppress her smile. "Mary Gannon will have all sorts of questions if she sees you escorting me to her front door."

"It's about time you and Declan come clean about this, you know. I live in fear that you'll be railroaded by the staunch Irish Mammy and be wed to her son in the church of her choice next week."

She lets out a loud laugh. "Not likely," she says. "Go now. I'm fine. I'll see you tomorrow somehow. I miss you all."

"We miss you too," I reply and then let her go, watching her make her way to the door and only pulling away when she is safely inside.

Chapter Twenty-Two

Ruby

"Hey," I say, coming face-to-face with Cillian as soon as I enter the house.

"How are you?" he asks straight away.

"I'm...good," I say with a smile. "Better than I have been for a while."

"Good, that's good," he says, acting agitated.

"What's up?" I ask cautiously.

"Did you talk to the men? Clear things up?" he asks.

"I did," I reply.

"Can we talk then?"

I nod. "Let me just go and say hi to your mom first."

"*Queever* is here too," he says.

I grimace. "Okay. How the fuck do you spell that?" I whisper.

He snorts and rolls his eyes at me. "C-a-o-i-m-h-e," he spells out.

"Fuck's sake," I mutter.

"Never mind that. You already know how to pronounce it, which is far more than any other non-Irish get. Hurry up. I'll wait upstairs for you."

He takes the stairs two at a time. I wonder what has him so eager. He must be dying to get in on this non-action that I've got going on. I purse my lips and head towards the kitchen.

"Hi," I chirp.

"Oh, there you are," Mary says. "Cup of tea?"

"No, I'm fine thanks," I politely decline yet more tea. "I just wanted to let you know I was back."

"Cillian told us you'd be along shortly. Did you two have fun?"

"Mm-hm," I murmur and feel Caoimhe's eyes on me.

I look at her and her blue eyes, just like her brother's, are boring into me, her arms are folded, and she looks pissed.

Shit.

What did I do?

"I'll go and freshen up and be down later," I mutter.

Mary waves me off, but Caoimhe follows me out and steers me towards the front room. "I'm very protective of my little brother," she says to me. "Both of them. What are you playing at here?"

"Nothing," I defend myself lamely.

"Saw you with that other guy," she accuses. "Hurt Declan and you have me to deal with. He's been through enough. He doesn't need some fancy tart turning his head and then stabbing him in the heart when he isn't here. *And* I've heard you were out with Cillian earlier."

"Look, Caoimhe, it isn't what you think," I start, taking offense to the 'fancy tart' remark.

"No?" she snaps. "I won't have you coming in here and tearing my brothers to pieces."

"Let me explain," I say wearily. "Not that it is any of your business, but Declan is aware of Ramsey and the other way around. I'm not sneaking around. I'm involved with both of them."

Her big blue eyes go wide, and she flicks her long dark ponytail over her shoulder. "I know my brother, missy," she hisses, taking me back slightly with her vehemence. "He loves you and I can see with my own two eyes that it borders on obsession, but that's just Declan. He focuses on something with everything he's got because it's easier to control. There is no way he would accept you dating another man."

"You've got it all wrong. I'm not dating them separately. We are all together, plus two other men," I growl at her, getting pissed off with the judgment.

"What?" she asks, her mouth agape. "You have got to be joking! Does Mam know?"

"No, she doesn't..."

"Oh, for the love of Jaysus, is Cillian one of them?"

"No," I say, shaking my head. I fail to add *not yet* because that is just adding fuel to the fire. "All four of the men are happy with this arrangement and so am I. Don't go looking for trouble where there isn't any, got it?" I grit out, not taking this shit from anyone, even Declan's sister.

The glower that heads my way looks very familiar and it makes me miss Declan even more. "Got it," she says, tightly. "But if I hear one word from Declan about how you've hurt him, I'll be coming for you."

"I won't hurt him," I say and brush past her. "But I'm glad you've got his back."

I'm not angry with her for the way this conversation went. How could I be when all she is doing is looking out for her brother? Brothers, even.

I disappear into the hallway and then stop when she turns to me and asks, "What's it like, having all those men at the same time?"

I smile, but don't turn around. "Perfect," I murmur and

head up the stairs to have my talk with Cillian, however that will go.

Chapter Twenty-Three

Ruby

I find him in my bedroom, hovering by the dresser, fiddling with the hairbrush.

"So where's the flash car?" I ask as an icebreaker.

He looks up, his face grim. "Had to get rid of it," he says shortly, replacing the brush.

"Oh?" I ask. "Trouble?"

"Something like that, but it can wait. I need to know what happened after I dropped you off at the cottage."

"A lot," I mutter, intrigued about his problem rather than my own which makes a refreshing change. "Can we talk about it now?"

"We are," he says, giving me a quizzical look.

"No, the trouble," I say, shaking my head.

He sighs. "Please, Ruby, I'll get to that. What did the men say about what happened earlier?"

"I told them exactly what happened and they're okay with it. They know it was for my benefit and the fact that you were a perfect gentleman goes a long way with them."

"Even Declan?"

"Yeah, they're all on board with whatever this is. But *what* is this? I can't give you any guarantees that this will fall under the guidelines of a normal relationship."

"I didn't think so, and I wasn't expecting it, love," he says. "All I need to hear right now is that I have permission from you and all of the others to explore this connection that I can feel between us."

"You do," I say carefully. "But…"

"You don't need to say another word, Ruby. I get it. All I want is the opportunity to know you and if things develop from there, then we'll cross that bridge."

"You didn't let me finish," I say with a small smile. "But your words are reassuring. Thank you. What I was going to say is, you live here, and I live in Manchester. I have no plans to move here. So…how will that work?"

"I'm glad you asked that because as it turns out, I'm free to make a move across to your city. In fact, it's the preferable option," he adds under his breath.

I pounce like a lioness in wait. "Why?" I say quickly. "What has happened?"

"Let's just say, I seem to have pissed off the wrong people," he replies with a soft smile.

"Who would that be then?"

"More *person* than people," he amends. "And you don't want to know him, believe me."

"Try me," I say quietly, moving forward and taking his hand. I pull him towards the bed, and we sit down.

He draws in a deep breath and shakes his head. "The less you know, the better. But as of half an hour ago, I've gone underground."

"Should you be here then?" I ask, licking my lips, in fear not for myself, but for his mom and sister.

"I wasn't followed," he says confidently. "I know how to shake a tail."

"That's why you ditched the Ferrari," I murmur.

"Yep."

"Declan said he'd be a couple more days. When he gets back, we're going home."

He nods. "I can make that work. I have money that I need to move around."

"Do you have anyone you can still trust?"

"Tadgh," he replies.

A slice of ice slides down my spine at his name. "Mm," I murmur.

"I should go. I'll see you in two days," he says, standing up. I stand as well.

"I'm worried about you," I say worriedly. "Is there anything I can do?"

"Just make sure you have somewhere for me in England. I'm no good at sitting on my arse doing nothing."

I nod slowly, an idea forming in my head already. I don't say anything though. This could potentially be huge, and I need to talk to the other men first, especially Declan. A thought occurs to me. "Do you know what Declan does?" I venture.

His eyes shoot to mine and go guarded. "Do you?" he asks carefully.

I nod.

He nods back and that is the end of that. I'm glad he knows how to protect his brother. There is no rivalry there that I can see and that will bode well. I'm still madly curious about the whole Siobhan thing, especially as their mom didn't seem to know about her and Cillian. Only her and Declan, but I suppose it will come out eventually. I can wait.

"Be safe," he murmurs, drawing me towards him and kissing the top of my head.

I'm getting a bit tired of that, but at the same time, I understand why they're doing it.

"When we get to England...is there unfinished business there?" he asks quietly.

"Declan took care of it," I mutter.

"Good. He would've suffered."

I hesitate to tell him the rest, but hey, he wants to know me, so I dive in. "The man who abducted me in the first place...*I* killed him. Stabbed him until he was nothing more than a sack of meat in a pool of blood. Still want to get involved?" I add lightly.

The heat in his eyes tells me all I need to know. He is as turned on by my vicious side as his twin is.

Works for me.

"Oh, yeah," he says. "Nothing sexier than a woman who knows how to handle herself."

I snort. "Yeah, look how far that got me, though."

"It got you free."

"True. Declan had to do the rest."

I nod and pull away from him, digging around in my bag for the black knife he lent me. "Want this back?" I ask, holding it out to him.

"Eventually. You keep it for now."

"I guess, I'll see you in a couple of days then," I say.

He smirks and leans forward to plant a kiss on my lips. "Do my kisses really suck?" he asks with a snort of laughter.

"Oh, please. If you're fishing for a compliment, don't bother. You know you made my knees weak. Just in a different way to Declan. That's good though. If it was the same, it would freak me out."

"You and me both," he mutters with a shudder.

We share a laugh and then he kisses me again chastely before he disappears into the night, leaving me considerably worried about him. At least I'm not worried about me, so it's something else to focus on. I hope he makes it back here in two days, or there is going to be hell to pay and not even the stench of my own fear will stop me from avenging him.

Let's just hope it doesn't come to that.

Chapter Twenty-Four

Declan

Three days was nowhere near enough time to complete this job. I needed a week to learn his habits, get to know his movements, figure out the best place to take him out. As it is, I've jumped on the first chance that presented itself, just so that I can get back to Ruby.

Not good for business, at all.

If I plan on keeping this up, I need to be able to leave her in the hands of the other men. For now, I can't leave. I will have to take a leave of absence from the killing business and when she's stronger, then I can come back to this. She is all I can think about. I can't focus on the job and that's going to end in disaster.

I stare down the scope of the rifle and wait, consumed by thoughts of Ruby. Ruby and Cillian, to be precise. I can't say that I'm thrilled about this new development, but I knew it would happen. He had way too much interest in her when I spoke about her, and he looks like me but does her job. There is no way she wouldn't be interested. I was in denial and trying to delay the inevitable. Now, here we are. However, the only thing that concerns me now is her state of mind. Is she doing this only because she is feeling vulnerable, or is it because she really wants to? I have absolutely no doubt in my mind that what transpired before was merely location based. Had she been with me, or one of the other men, it also would've happened. It has nothing to do with Cillian. He was just there, and she obviously trusts him. I *told* her she could, and she trusts me. So, while it rankles me, I'm not envious of the situation. She came looking for *me* afterwards. There is something between us that no one, not even my twin can come in between, and that is the way I intend for it to stay. I will defend my role with her to the death, and not give a flying crap if it is Cillian or someone else. No one takes her away from me.

No one.

Right now, this arsehole I'm waiting to shoot in the head is taking her away from me. Time to end it.

I see him round the corner, back from his lunch, right on time. Mere luck. I'm not spiritual. I don't believe that the universe handed him to me at this precise moment without any delays to his schedule just so I could get back to Ruby. It's not fate. It's just my good luck and his bad luck.

I inhale slowly and when I exhale, I pull the trigger. It's a breezeless day and the trajectory is bang on.

The bullet hits him right in the middle of his forehead.

I don't dally after seeing him go down. I sit up, dismantle the rifle and place it carefully into the case. I scoop up the shell casing and throw that in as well. I slam the lid shut and close the snaps briskly.

Picking it up, I head straight for the stairs and take them steadily, down the ten floors of the empty office building and out of the door, slipping out onto the street in the melee of the aftermath.

I have minutes to cross the park and get back to my car. The net is closing already by the time I reach the Range Rover, but no one pays any attention to me in my flat cap and duster coat. They are all too busy panicking at the incident that occurred a thousand yards away. I throw the case under the back seat and then climb in and drive off, heading straight for the border and back to Ruby.

My phone rings and I connect it to the Bluetooth speaker and answer. "Is it done?" I ask Aidan.

"Yeah, all sorted."

"Thanks," I mutter and hang up.

The brief call soothes my soul slightly about being away from Ruby. I know I will be back with her soon, and then we can get going.

I don't want to linger for too long. Mam is asking too many questions about Ruby and her accident, when am I going to ask her to marry me and give her grandkids. I know it isn't what Ruby wants. She has never mentioned it, but I know. I only want what is best for her, so I won't pressure her. I've never thought too much about all that stuff, so it doesn't bother me that she doesn't want any of that. With her life and mine, it makes no sense anyway.

I don't know how the other men feel, but Cillian vowed never to marry again after the disaster with Siobhan. If the others can't accept that Ruby isn't cut out for that life, then they will have to readjust their thinking with a little help from me. I won't have any of them putting pressure on or making her feel guilty for her choices.

In retrospect, I don't think any of them would, but you never know. Maybe it's a deal breaker for one of them. In which case, I'll make a deal with breaking their arm. Simple.

. . .

I drive the rest of the way, focused only on getting back to Ruby. I cross the border into Ireland, my heart aching to see her. Never again will I be this long away from her. Next time, she comes with me where I can make sure she is safe and happy. I know deep down it is impractical, but it makes me feel better thinking that way.

When I pull up into Mam's driveway, I hastily turn off the engine and get out of the car, stalking to the door. It opens before I get there and Ruby comes flying out, flinging her arms around me and kissing me sweetly.

"Missed you, Daddy," she murmurs, setting my body alight. "I need you."

"What have you done?" I ask carefully, trying not to let her words cut me. I don't know the deal yet. It could be nothing.

But it could be something.

"Kept a secret," she says and pulls away from me to enter the house again. I follow her quickly, closing the door and hoping Mam isn't around.

I see Ruby head up the stairs, so I take them two at a time, right behind her.

When she disappears into her bedroom, I follow and shut the door on the rest of the world.

Chapter Twenty-Five

Ruby

It has taken every ounce of courage that I have to do this. I'm scared, but I'm powering through. There is no option but to keep moving forward. I know I made the right choice when Declan's face lit up. He needs this and I want to give it to him.

"What secrets have you kept, Princess?" he murmurs, curling my hair behind my ear.

I reach up and tug on his belt, undoing it and slowly pulling it out of the loops.

He watches me with hooded eyes, desire filling them even though I can see he is trying to squash it for me. It makes me love him.

I fall hard and fast and it makes this easier.

Deep down, I know it's not just for him. It's for me as well. The first time I was raped it took me *years* to get over it. I'm not willing to accept that this time. I have men in my life who I know will wait, but that's not fair. I don't want them to hang around wondering if today will be the day I let them touch me. Or tomorrow, or never. It scares me that I may lose them, but that's not the driving force behind this bold move that has made my stomach twist into a knot.

It's a small step, and it's for me to take back control and not let this keep me down. I know how to deal with it. The first time was bad, the memories nearly killed me. But this time was different. I barely remember it. It was over with so quickly and I felt nothing. I believe I'm more traumatized by the injections that Boomer used to torture me and the stabbing and being left to bleed out.

I give the belt a tug. It falls free from the last loop, and I hold it up. Declan's hand clamps around my wrist.

I don't flinch.

"Tell Daddy what you did," he whispers, taking the belt from me and wrapping it around his fist.

I shiver.

I'm both equal parts afraid and aroused.

It's a feeling that I have never experienced before and it's intoxicating.

"I kept a secret," I pout.

"What kind of secret?"

"I should've told you all, but I didn't."

"You can tell me now, Princess. I want to hear what you've been keeping from me."

His tone is darkly delicious, and I just fall into it. I don't think. I don't feel. I just act. I play the role of his Princess and he eats it up.

"I was a bad girl, Daddy. Can you forgive me?"

"Perhaps," he says.

The lack of confirmation sends a tremor through my body. I drop to my knees and bow my head.

"Princess," he rasps. "Stand up."

"No, Daddy. I must confess."

"What is there to confess?"

"I thought I was pregnant," I whisper, forcing the words through my lips. I need him to know. I need all of them to know.

Silence.

I know what he's thinking. It's obvious without even looking up.

"Oh?" he croaks.

"I was scared. I didn't want anyone to know in case it was *his*," I whimper.

"And?"

"I took a test. It came back negative. I'm so relieved, Daddy, but I knew if I was that I'd have to have an abortion and I hate that I wouldn't have had a choice."

"So you're not...?" he asks.

He sounds terrified.

"No," I whisper.

"Why did you keep this to yourself?" he asks slowly. "You could've told us. We are here to help you, Princess."

"I know. But I didn't want to see the fear on your faces if it came back positive. I didn't trust you to not abandon me."

"Oh, Ruby," he cries and drops to his knees in front of me. "Don't you know by now that we would never leave. None of us. I have killed for you, and I'd kill again and again to keep you safe. I'd die for you. You don't ever have to be afraid to tell me anything."

"Do you forgive me?"

I swear to God, if he says there's nothing to forgive, I'll claw his eyes out.

But he knows better than that.

"Yes, Princess," he says, leaning forward to kiss my forehead.

Grrrrrr.

"Kiss me like you mean it," I snarl at him.

"No, I can't." He shakes his head.

"Kiss me now," I demand. "I need it. I need to feel your lips on mine. I need to see if..."

I stop speaking, knowing my next words will hurt.

"See what?" he asks cautiously.

"I need to see if I can get aroused. Please, Daddy, kiss me."

His blue eyes fill with sadness, but he cups the back of my head and presses his lips to mine. He sweeps his tongue over my lips, and I open up, allowing him to plunge his tongue into my mouth.

"Princess," he growls, shuffling closer. "Do you feel how much I love you?"

I do. I can feel a teeny, tiny spark deep inside me that has lit up at his kiss. It's not much, but it's something.

"Yes," I whisper against his lips, cupping his face and trying to force a bigger reaction. He starts to pant when I ravage his mouth and crawl into his lap.

I'm desperate to do this. Desperate to feel normal again and have sex with a man I care about. I *need* to have someone else be the last man inside me and not *him*.

I feel his hands go still on my arms and he stops kissing me. "Ruby..."

"No talking. Just kiss me," I mumble.

I can feel his erection bursting to get to me, but he pushes me gently away. "I'm not doing that," he says firmly.

"Why not?" I snap. "You want me. That much is obvious."

"For all my sins, Princess, I know I'm a better man than that with you. Don't ask me to be an arsehole for you. I won't. I can't. And it'll just piss me off."

"I need to see if I can do this!" I shout at him, feeling the frustration tearing at my soul. I beat my hands on his chest, tears streaming down my face.

He grabs my fists and kisses them. "Ruby. You don't need to prove anything to anyone."

"It's not about that. I don't want him to be the last man to have been with me!"

Okay. I didn't want to say that. I wanted to keep that thought to myself. It's not fair. I don't want him to only do it because of that. I need him to want to do it.

"Fuck, Ruby," he says desperately. "Fuck!"

He pushes me away and stands up, starting to pace with his hands over his eyes. "Fuck!" He roars and smashes his fist into the wall.

"Jaysus fecking Christ!" He slams his fist again and again into the wall, until he's bleeding all over the carpet.

I don't move a muscle. I can't. I'm frozen in place. I feel so guilty now, I need to start this all over and ask for absolution for putting this on him.

"I'm so-sorry," I stammer. "Forget I said..."

He lets out a noise of sheer torment and in two giant strides, he bends down and sweeps me off my feet, cradling me against him.

He lays me down on the bed and I freeze. My heart is hammering in my chest.

"Tell me to stop," he begs me, unzipping my jeans. "Please, Ruby, tell me to stop."

I shake my head.

"Fuck, Ruby." He squeezes his eyes shut and undoes his pants. They drop around his ankles and he leans over me to pull my jeans further down.

"Tell me to stop," he grits out, opening his eyes to show me his tears.

"Do it," I beg him. "Please do it. I need you, Daddy. I need you to take care of this for me."

"Damn you, Ruby. Damn you!" he snarls and drops down on top of me. He kisses me roughly, pinning me to the bed with his weight. I wiggle underneath him to lower my jeans so he can do this. They're stuck around the middle of my thighs, and I can barely open my legs, but he takes his cock in his hand and guides it into me as gently as he can under the circumstances and his intense frustration and pain for doing this.

I open up as much as I can as he thrusts deeply inside me, once, twice, three times.

I cry out in anguish, lying still and inactive in this painful, awkward sex that I've forced him into by placing all the responsibility on him to get rid of this feeling.

"Ruby," he pants. "Is it enough? Can I stop? Please, please. I can't do this…"

He pulls out of me and drops to his knees on the floor, his face on my thighs, soaking them with his tears.

I run my hand into his hair, my own tears sliding out of the sides of my eyes and onto the bed covers.

"It's enough. Thank you, Daddy. Thank you," I murmur with a relief that makes me go dizzy and weak. "Thank you."

Chapter Twenty-Six

Ruby

I don't know how long we lay like that. Quite some time. Eventually, he stands and pulls his pants up. Then he undresses me tenderly and settles me in my comfy sweats and vest top.

Once I'm in bed, snuggled under the duvet, he strokes my face and with a sad smile, he turns towards the door.

"Stay," I say, needing him not to leave me.

He turns back and climbs on the bed, over the covers and takes me in his arms.

"Are you okay?" I ask after a minute of courage gathering.

He peers down at me. "Yes. I'm more concerned for you."

"I'm okay. I just mean, you know, you didn't finish..." I bite my lip and trail off.

He chuckles. "Oh, don't worry about me, Princess. Nothing a wank won't sort later."

I giggle. "Wank," I choke out. "Such a funny word."

He snickers. "I'm used to that anyway. Every time I saw you in Giselle's, before you knew who I was, I would have to go and have a wank, thinking about you and wanting so badly to tell you that I knew you."

"I was so attracted to you. I wish you had told me sooner," I murmur.

"I do too. I was scared, I guess. It was easier to be a ghost."

Holding onto the courage, I say, "I can take care of it for you."

"No," he says adamantly. "You don't need to do that."

"Are you sure?"

"Yes," he states, and his tone is final, so I drop it.

I then broach the subject that I've been dreading for the last two days. "Uhm, about Cillian," I start but then have nowhere to go with it.

"What about him?" he asks.

"Have you spoken to him in the last couple of days?"

"Yes. He rang to ask for the details of the flight out tomorrow," he replies, in just as cautious a tone as me.

"And did you give it to him?"

"Of course," he says, with a laugh.

"Did he sound okay?" I venture.

"He's in trouble, you know that much," he says with a sigh. "He didn't give many details, just that you two had reached an agreement that he would come to England to lay low for a bit."

"Is that all right with you?"

"Yes, Ruby. We've had this conversation."

"I know, but I'm triple-checking. I don't want there to be any weirdness between the two of you."

"There won't be," he assures me.

I can't help but wonder why he is so confident. Have they done this before? Shared a woman? This Siobhan, maybe?

"Do you plan on going back to work right away?" he asks, changing the subject.

"Yeah," I say with a sigh. "I mean your mom is lovely and

so generous, and she's been a much-needed source of comfort, but I'm bored out of my skull. Is that okay with you?"

"What does it have to do with me?" he asks, perplexed.

"Everything. You and the other men. I'll be going back into it all. I don't want you to worry."

"That is a given, Princess," he says. "Even if this hadn't happened, I'd be worried constantly about you. This world is dangerous and going back to Manchester to reclaim your place, especially now that Jake is gone and there are skirmishes to take over his place, I can't not worry about you. But I won't stop you. I know how much blood, sweat and tears you've put into your work. Just don't ask me not to worry because that will never happen."

His words have piqued my interest. I sit up and regard him closely. "You're saying no one has taken over yet?"

He shakes his head. "Aidan is there, keeping an eye on the situation. He says it's volatile, but as of yet, nothing has been decided."

"Perfect," I murmur.

"Ruby," he says, also sitting up. "You aren't thinking of going for it yourself, are you?"

"No," I say, shaking my head and hoping he doesn't see the small lie. "I'm just curious."

"Ruby," he warns me, telling me that he does know I'm hiding something.

"I don't want it," I state firmly, but neglect to tell him that I plan on backing Cillian for the job. Whatever trouble he is in, whoever it is won't mess with an entire organization. Out on his own, Cillian is a sitting duck, but this way he will be protected. I haven't thought it all the way through yet, and that's why I don't want to say anything. I was working on the assumption that I would have to oust another asshole from the head of the snake, but this is easier. Much, much easier.

It couldn't be more perfect if I'd planned it. The factions

will be so busy fighting each other, that they won't even notice that Cillian has slid in until it's too late.

I lie back down with a smile on my face and close my eyes.

This night has been hell to get through, but I got through it, and now I plan on taking back everything that is rightfully mine, and then some.

The city had better watch out.

The Black Widow is back.

Chapter Twenty-Seven

Ruby

I didn't seem to be asleep that long when I'm woken up by my phone vibrating on the nightstand. I groan and open my eyes, pleased to see that not only did Declan stay, but he is also sleeping. However, it doesn't last long, when I lean over him to grab my phone.

"What? Fuck? What?" he says, sitting upright and knocking the phone out of my hand.

"David," I say, retrieving it from the tangled bed sheets.

"Oh," he says, rubbing his face. "Fuck, I haven't slept like that...ever..."

"Must be me," I reply lightly with a smile and then answer the video call. "What's up?" I ask, suddenly getting a sliver of cold down my spine. David's face is grim.

"Hey, listen, we can't leave today. We can't go back home yet," he says calmly but firmly.

"Why not?" I ask with a frown.

"What's happened?" Declan demands, practically shoving me out of the way so he can see David on the screen.

"Do you mind?" I grumble and shove him back a bit so that half our faces are visible to David on the other side.

"The police have swung by Widows looking for you," David says.

"Why?" I ask quietly.

"They found your card in..." he pauses and then growls out, "*Smith's* stuff at the station, plus the statement from the last time he came by after you were attacked by Jake's guy. They want to talk to you as a person of interest in Smith's disappearance, according to the Banker. Who, BTDubs, is not impressed he's had to deal with the po-po in your absence."

"Fuck," I groan and exchange a wary look with Declan. "What does this mean?"

"It means, we stay here for a bit longer until I can figure something out," Declan says, and then looks towards the door when there is a loud, official sounding knock on the front door downstairs.

"Shit," he mumbles and leaps off the bed.

In fight or flight mode, I pick flight and jump up, dragging my bag out from under the bed. I start throwing clothes into it as Declan comes back and confirms my worst fears.

"It's the *Garda*," he says.

"Who is that banging on my door at this hour?" Mary calls from her room down the hallway.

"Fuck, fuck, fuck," I mutter. "Can they arrest me? It's a different country. I don't know the rules..." I start to not exactly panic, but it's definitely got the adrenaline going.

"We don't know they are here for you. They might be here about Cillian," Declan says, but ruins his half-assed reassurance by helping me throw stuff into the bag. "We have to get out of here."

"No shit," I hiss as Mary's footsteps sound outside the door and then go down the stairs.

"Mam, wait," Declan calls out and follows her.

I yank my shoes on, grateful that I'm in 'running-away' clothes and drag my coat on.

"Rubes? Rubes? What is going on?" David's muffled voice is coming from the bed somewhere.

I pull the covers back and snatch up the phone. "Trouble," I mutter and scooping up my bag, I follow Declan down the stairs.

"It's the *Garda*," Declan is explaining to his mom in a whisper.

"Who are they here for? You or her?" she asks.

I grimace. This is going to hell in a handbasket.

"Don't know," Declan mutters. "But we need you to stall them, please."

She nods grimly. "If I didn't do that a hundred times for your da back in the day. I know how to stall. Head out the back, and straight down the garden to the gate at the bottom. It leads out onto the field, and you can get to the woods from there," she says all commandery.

I'm impressed.

Declan nods and grabs a pair of boots from near the door as the banging starts to get more insistent and yanks them onto his feet.

"Hold yer damn horses!" Mary calls out.

Declan grabs me by the elbow and gives his mom a quick kiss. "Thank you," he says and steers me away.

"Take care of your girl, Declan," she insists quietly, causing me to turn around in surprise. I thought she'd be mad and disappointed in me.

All I see is understanding and a determination to protect me at all costs.

"Thank you for everything," I murmur.

She nods grimly, and then shoos us away.

"What the fuck is going on?" David yells out and I shush

him as Declan leads me out of the back door, across the garden to the gate that will lead to our escape.

I hope.

I've seen the movies, where the cops are lying in wait at your supposed exit.

But luckily, there is no one ready to ambush us. We make our getaway through the field and into the small woods.

"What now?" I ask Declan.

"There's a shed about a mile into the woods. I have a car stashed."

"Of course you do," David drawls from the phone I'm still clutching in my hand.

Declan takes my bag from me. "Can you keep up?" he asks me.

"Set the pace and I'll do my best," I say, slightly out of breath already. Failure to hit the gym for coming on a month now is definitely showing. My side is protesting, but I ignore it and keep up. He is moving swiftly, but steadily, so I look down at David.

"Are you up to speed?" I ask.

"Irish pigs at the door, you're fleeing, Mama G defending the stronghold," he says, counting it out on his fingers.

I snort. "Guess you are."

"Where are you going?" he asks.

I shrug. "You need to get ready to head out," I mutter, knowing they'll already be packed because we were meant to leave today anyway. I got sidetracked by my night with Declan and packing was forgotten.

"Get in the car and head west," Declan calls out, taking the phone from me. I stumble and Declan stops, dropping my bag and holding me steady.

"I'm okay," I mumble.

"We'll have a minute," he says and then goes back to barking instructions to Layton now on where to go.

"County Galway," he says, "Head towards Connemara."

"Got it," Layton says and hands the phone back to David. Declan passes it to me. "Why there?" I ask.

"It's fairly remote and I have a safe house there," he says. "If Cillian has his ear to the ground, which I suspect he will, he'll meet us there."

"But he doesn't know we aren't going back to England…"

"If the *Garda* is at the door, trust me, he knows I wouldn't risk air travel."

"Okay," I say, hoping he's right.

He gives me a reassuring smile and that's when it hits me. The thrill of this is affecting me in a big way. I thrive on the danger and darkness my world brings, and this has thrown me right back into the middle of it and then some. My adrenaline spikes and I feel alive. My silent proclamation earlier comes into full force and it's not only the Black Widow who is back, but me as well.

"Declan," I rasp when he turns to pick up my bag again.

"We need to move, Princess," he says. "Can you manage?"

I nod, but then I hang up the phone and throw it onto the bag still on the ground. "Take me," I whisper.

"What?" he asks, going still.

"Right here, right now, take me," I pant, moving into his arms and undoing his pants. His belt is still on the floor of my room, so access is easy to let his pants drop open.

"No," he says, his hands clamping around my wrists. "Not again. Not like that."

Shaking my head, I say, "This is different. This is real. I need *you*, Declan."

"Fuck, Ruby," he groans and lets go of my wrists. I think he is about to do up his pants again when his hands clamp around my upper arms. With a low growl, he spins me and shoves me up against the nearest tree. "You had better say *now* if you don't want this."

"I want this," I purr, clutching his shirt and dragging him closer. "I need you."

"I know what this is," he hisses. "You are thriving on the danger, the chase. You're aroused by the thought of getting caught out here in the middle of the woods with my cock buried deep inside you."

"Fuuuck," I moan and bruise my own lips, I kiss him so hard.

I am currently devoid of any thoughts. I'm just feeling and right now, his words have hit the mark dead on. This is the old me. The Black Widow might've made a comeback last night, but Ruby was still cowering slightly.

Not anymore.

He devours my mouth, his hands tightening on my arms. "Last chance," he rasps. "I can't stop once I'm inside you. Not this time. Not again."

"Don't stop," I murmur and gasp when he lets go of my arms and drags my sweats down. He pulls one of my shoes off and releases my left leg from its confinement. Then he clamps his hands on my ass and lifts me up, shoving me back up against the tree forcefully.

I inhale, closing my eyes.

Big mistake.

All I can see now is Smith looming over me, rolling the condom over his cock...

"No!" I shout out, opening my eyes.

Declan freezes, his cock at my entrance. "Fuck, Ruby, I knew...I knew..."

"No!" I say quickly. "Not you. Keep going. Look into my eyes. Say my name."

"Ruby," he purrs in that sexy accent. "Oh, Ruby."

He thrusts deeply and I moan, his dark blue eyes boring into mine, never breaking contact as he fucks me slowly, against this tree.

"Declan," I pant, clasping my hands around the back of his neck. "Yes, that's it!" I cry out, elated that I can feel the pleasure zooming through my body.

Last night was awful. I wasn't turned on at all. I just needed the imprint of Smith's cock out of my pussy. With that gone, with Declan, a man that I love, erasing that for me and replacing it with his own, it healed me quicker than two agonizing years last time.

My clit twitches and I soak Declan's cock. He groans when he feels it and thrusts harder, faster, digging his fingers into my ass cheeks.

"You feel so good," he pants. "Fuck, Ruby, you do things to me that I've never felt before. I love you. I love you. I love... uhn..." He thrusts high and deep, and I feel it. I feel my pussy clench around his cock as he spurts his load, flooding me with his cum.

"Yes!" I cry out as the climax rips through me. "Declan!"

He grabs my hair in his fist and kisses me roughly. Biting my lips, sucking my tongue, consuming me.

He pulls back, leaning his forehead against mine as he regains his breath. "Are you okay?" he murmurs.

"Yes, I promise I'm just fine," I say with a smile and then burst out laughing as the tension is broken.

I jump a mile when David's voice rings out in the middle of the woods. "RUDE!" He bellows, but then laughs.

"David?" I ask, wiggling out of Declan's hold on me.

"Down here," he says. "You didn't exactly hang up the phone then, Ruby."

"Oh, God!" I cry and snatch up the phone before I even pull my sweats back up. "David!" I bite my lip as his beautiful hazel eyes peer back at me from the phone screen.

"I'm so glad," he says quietly. "My heart is filled with happiness for you that you took back what was taken from you. You deserve to have everything your heart desires, including a beautiful sex life with the man who loves you more than anything in this world."

"And you," I choke back the sob that bubbles up. "All of you. I'm sorry. I should've waited, but the feeling was there, and I snatched it up."

"So you should have," Ramsey says, taking the phone from David. "Don't worry for one second about us. We are happy that you took the risk and you got what you needed."

"Are you sure?" I ask, letting Declan help me back on with my sweats and shoe.

"Of course," Layton says, although I can't see him because he is driving.

It reminds me we need to get on the road immediately. We have lingered for far too long in this one spot.

"I love you," I say suddenly. "David, Ramsey, Layton, I love each of you so much."

"And we love you," David says, showing his face again. "Now get back to your escaping, like, right the hell now," he instructs and then hangs up. For real this time.

"And me?" Declan asks, stooping to pick my bag up.

I grab his hand and kiss it. "I love you, Declan. You have brought me back to myself, not once, but twice. I owe you everything."

"No," he says. "You have done that yourself. Your strength and courage to reclaim your life is all yours, Ruby. I do love you more than anything else in this world, so can we get going now? I don't want to lose you if we get caught."

I nod, my throat too thick with emotion to speak and we pick up the pace again until I see the shed and breathe out in relief.

Declan ushers me inside and pops the trunk, throwing my bag into it. He opens the passenger door of the nondescript white sedan and I climb in. Once he is settled in the driver's side and turns on the ignition, a head pops up from the back seat in between us, stopping my heart and making me scream.

Chapter Twenty-Eight

Cillian

"What in the name of hell fire are you doing?" Declan barks at me.

"What the feck does it look like?" I reply. "Hitching a ride."

"Jesus!" Ruby screams in my face. "You nearly gave me a heart attack."

"Sorry," I say with a soft smile, wanting to reach out and touch her more than anything, but I don't. She has been through enough and I am not in the business of throwing myself at women.

Well, not anymore. Once bitten and all that.

She returns my smile. "I'm happy to see you're still alive, but how did you know we would come here?" she asks.

"Easy. I know my brother."

She glances between us as Declan growls and pulls out of the shed, getting out of the car and closing the doors before he gets back in.

"You were supposed to meet us in Connemara," Declan says.

"Yeah, I know, but getting rid of my wheels was making that a pain in the arse. So who was the *Garda* there for? You, me or her?" I ask with a snort.

"We don't know. Mam took care of it," Declan says.

"Probably you," Ruby states huffily and turns around. She is worried though. I can see that plain as day.

"Hmm, possibly," I murmur.

"Who did you piss off?" she asks, turning around again as Declan bounces over the dirt track in the woods to make it to the road that will lead out onto the main road.

I grimace. "Long story."

"Road trip…we've got time," she retorts.

She has such sass. I find it quite arousing. Siobhan had sass. Not as much as Ruby, but I loved that about her. She didn't take shit from anyone. I ruminate that I have a type. Strong woman.

"Hello?" Ruby calls out, waving her hand in my face.

"Hm? Sorry…yeah…okay. My boss."

"And?" she asks.

I pause to take in the glow on her cheeks, the spark in her eyes. She is worlds away from the fragile creature of only a few days ago. I want to ask why, but I can see how my brother is acting. He has his hand possessively on hers unless he has to turn or change gears, but then it goes straight back. Whatever has brought her fire back, he has something to do with it.

"And, he is a gobshite that you don't want to mess with."

"So why did you?"

I snort. "Didn't have much choice there, love," I retort.

"For the love of Jaysus, just spit it out," Declan snarls at me. "Ruby hates beating around the bush."

"Hm, reminds me of someone," I murmur.

"Siobhan?" Ruby snaps. "You're thinking about her, aren't you?"

"Jealous?" I taunt her with a laugh, glad that we have changed the topic. I really don't want to tell her why I've had to go underground.

"Pah!" she hisses. "You wish. I'm not jealous of any whore you've dipped your wick in."

"Oh, ouch," I comment and sit back, leaning my head against the headrest.

"Look," Ruby says, exhaling loudly. "I get that you both loved this woman. But if you are going to be thinking about her while you are with me, you can fuck right off. Did you share her? Hm? Did you both fuck her at the same time?"

"How long have you been sitting on that?" Declan asks, almost in disbelief.

"A while," she growls. "I was waiting to have you both here to ask."

"The answer is no. We didn't. You will be the first," he replies softly, giving her what I could only call a brave smile. "When you are ready, of course. Does that satisfy your curiosity, Princess?"

"Yes, I guess so," she grouses.

"Princess?" I ask. "Is that because you're like a billionaire or whatever?" I ask, scrunching up my nose. It's not fair. I want to give her a cutesy pet name.

She laughs loudly. "You mistake my parent's wealth for my own. No, I'm not a billionaire. I grew up with rich parents, that's it."

"But you're heiress to the family fortune, no?" I probe.

"Why are you so interested?" she asks suspiciously, giving me the stink-eye. "You only here for the money?"

"Hardly," I scoff, "And you know it. Just curious, is all."

"Humph," she mutters. "He calls me Princess because he is my Daddy," she adds, giving me a smug smile.

I feel my cheeks heat up and I splutter. "What?"

"Ruby," Declan exclaims. "Why are you telling him that?"

"He doesn't know about that side of you?" she asks incredulously. "Hahaha," she snorts with laughter which is infectious.

"Uhm, yeah, you're going to have to explain that to me," I state.

"I will, *after* you tell us why you had to go underground," she says.

"Feck's sake," I mutter. "Like a dog with a bone."

She smirks at me, and I feel my own bone stiffen in my pants. She is a dirty little thing. It's surprising. I figured she was a sex goddess, but in a more 'vanilla' way. I curse myself for thinking about her in that way. What she has been through…I owe her more respect than that.

"Cillian," Declan says when I stay silent. "She will keep asking. You might as well be transparent. It will also do us well to know exactly what you are running from in case we need to run again because of you."

I sigh and run my hand through my hair. The seriousness of this finally gets through to her, and she frowns.

"Why don't you want to tell me?" she asks.

"Because it has to do with you," I say eventually, wishing that she'd just left it.

"Me," she asks in surprise. "What could I have possibly done to your boss holed up in your mom's house?"

I need to tell her that *she* is the one I've given up my entire business for.

Declan has gone still. He knows something is up.

"Connor knows who you are," I start. "There are associates in the organization who know you as the Black Widow. When he knew you'd been by the warehouse the other day, he ordered me to…" I stop, finding this difficult to get out.

Will it trigger her in some way? I have no way of knowing how she will react.

"To what?" Declan grits out.

"Take you out," I say quietly, staring into her eyes.

She blinks once and then turns back to face the front of the car for the first time since we set off. "I see," she says tightly. She pulls her hand out of Declan's and fists both of them in her lap.

"I refused, obviously," I say, sitting forward again. "And he took offense. Said it was you or me. I chose me. I ditched the Ferrari, took as much cash as I could fit into this bag..." I pat the big black holdall next to me on the seat, "and went underground."

"Why did he want me gone?" she asks after a weighted pause.

"He has been trying to find a foothold over the sea," I explain. "You pretty much dropped into his lap. He figured taking you out would let him slide into your operation in Manchester and take it over, then the rest and then the city."

"Thinks quite highly of himself, doesn't he?" she asks with a trace of humor, which eases my anxiety a bit over telling her. My stomach is still in knots. I'm not as cold as Declan. Don't get me wrong, I will gut you like a fish if the need arises, but in the times where the adrenaline isn't pounding through me, I suffer with anxiety and panic attacks. It has everything to with the abuse our da handed out on a daily basis. Declan took the brunt of it, defending me as my older brother, albeit by two minutes. He made sure Caoimhe was protected and dealt with the sexual abuse instead of her. I tried to...once. I thought I was going to die. I have no idea how Declan managed to take on so much and not curl up and end it some days.

I turn my head, tears pricking my eyes as the horror of our childhood rises up and I try to steady my breathing.

"Cillian," Ruby says softly, bringing me back slightly.

"You gave up everything for me? Why? Why didn't you just tell me, and we could have left sooner?"

I shake my head. "When Connor gets an idea in his head, he won't shake it until it's done. You are still in danger. Just not from me. Never from me."

I hear the click of her seatbelt and then she clambers into the back of the car with me. I scoot over, shoving the bag on the floor so she can curl up next to me. She takes me in her arms and rests her head on my shoulder.

In that moment, without any words between us, I know I love her. She has put me first and the only other person to do that my entire life was Declan. She isn't stressing that she is on the Irish mob's hit list. She is worried about the effect this is having on me.

"You're sweet," I murmur, turning my head towards her so that I can kiss her forehead. "Don't worry about me. I'll survive. Always do."

"But you ruined your whole life just to protect me," she points out and cups my face.

"Not many people would do that."

"Ahem," Declan mutters from the front.

She giggles. "I said 'not many'," she chides him. "I know you would burn the world down to save me."

"Fucking right, I would," he murmurs.

"So would I," I say, not that I'm trying to compete. I just want her to know. The small time that I've known her, she has gotten under my skin in a way that no woman ever has.

She rests her head on my shoulder and we sit in silence for about an hour, then her phone rings and disturbs the peace we had fallen into.

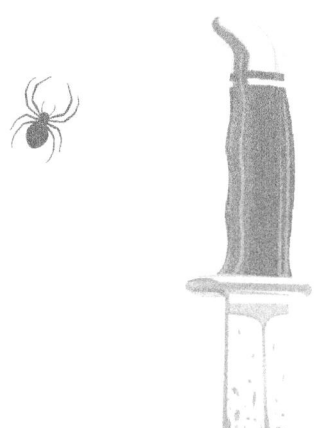

Chapter Twenty-Nine

Layton

After David called twenty minutes ago, we finally see the white sedan pull up next to us on the side of the road in a beautifully scenic spot on the west coast of Ireland. I have traveled to many places, but most were dusty, hot, had no views to speak of and were with the Armed Forces. I have taken the time to appreciate this while we waited for Ruby to catch up.

Declan pulls up and she leaps out, running over to me and throwing her arms around me. I engulf her, almost crushing her, but needing to show her how happy I am to see her and know that she is turning a corner. I shove her up against the car and claim her mouth in a kiss that becomes so erotic, I feel my dick harden and strain against my black combat pants.

Panting, she pulls away and smiles at me, a bright, sexy smile that reassures me she is fine after I nearly devoured her.

"Hi," she says, pushing me away slightly and once we are clear of the car, the door at the back opens and Cillian climbs out.

I snicker and shake my head. "I see," I murmur. "Kept that quiet, didn't you?"

She grins and leaves me to greet David and Ramsey in much the same way.

I give Declan a nod, but step in front of him so he can't duck around me. "About what happened earlier," I start.

He holds his hand up. "Look, it wasn't as random as it looked to you. Last night…" he sighs, and it catches Ruby's attention. She is holding hands with David and drags him closer, biting her lip.

"Go on," I growl. "Last night, what?"

"I asked Daddy to take care of something for me," Ruby says.

"I want to hear from him," I grit out, pointing at Declan.

"You sure you want to do this on the side of the road?" he spits out.

"Yes," I state, folding my arms over my chest. If he went near her without her permission, I would kill him regardless of who he is.

"Fine," Declan says, meeting my steady gaze with one of his own, but it is etched with torment.

What the fuck happened?

"Ruby came to me with a secret she has been keeping. Something she needed to get off her chest. She asked for forgiveness, and I gave it to her in the way which we both know she needs. Then she spilled something far, far worse that tore at my heart. Ruby?" he asks, looking at her. "Do I have your permission to tell them?"

"Yes, of course," she murmurs, looking at the ground.

I clench my jaw so tight, it aches. I knew something was going on but had no idea what. Now, I'm starting to think this was a bad idea, but the masochist in me needs to hear it.

"We don't have to do this here," David says, pulling her closer.

"Yes, we do," she mutters. "I thought I might be pregnant," she adds quietly. "I took a test, but it came back negative. That was a few days ago. I didn't tell any of you because I was scared that if I was and it turned out to be his, you would leave me."

"Jesus, Ruby," I chide her, going to her and pulling her back into my arms. "You know we would never do that."

She snuffles against my chest, and I squeeze her tighter until she chokes back a laugh. "Can't breathe," she says.

"Sorry," I mutter and let her go.

She smiles sadly, but keeps her arms around me, her head on my chest. "Declan, can you tell them the rest? I don't think I can…"

He inhales. His face is hard when he says, "Ruby and I kissed. It was deep, but I knew something was off. She crawled into my lap, and I pushed her away. That's when she revealed what has been plaguing her all these weeks. She said…" He swallows visibly and Ruby turns her head into my chest. "…she said that she needed me to have sex with her, so she didn't have to feel him inside her anymore."

"Fuck," I mutter. "Ruby…why didn't you tell us before?"

"Because I was humiliated and disgusted and drowning in self-pity," comes her muffled reply, her head still against me.

"Rubes," David says, taking her and turning her so he can wrap his arms around her. He doesn't say anything else, because what is there to say? We can't tell her that she shouldn't feel that way. It will invalidate what is so real to her.

"And did you?" I ask Declan tightly.

"Yes," he croaks out. "It was an act to erase what she was feeling. Nothing more."

"It was awful!" she cries out.

Declan grunts and looks away.

"I mean, the whole thing was a living nightmare," she tries

to make it better, but somehow ends up making it sound worse.

"I know it wasn't my finest performance, Princess, but living nightmare?" Declan says, rallying himself enough to give her a smirk.

She laughs. "I'm sorry, I don't mean you, I mean the whole thing. But it worked, and I felt nothing but relief. It was over so fast..." She bites her lip.

"I couldn't do it for longer than about three seconds," Declan adds.

I breathe in deeply through my nose and then out through my mouth. "There was no reason for you to feel so alone," I say to Ruby. "You should have talked to us about this."

"I know," she says. "I wanted to, but I just couldn't bring myself to say the words."

Ramsey takes her other hand and then I turn to Cillian, still leaning up against the car, staying out of this private conversation.

"So, you're Cillian," I say, changing the subject from this painful one. I will discuss it further with Ruby when we are alone. Right now, she has been through enough.

"Yep," he says.

"I'm Layton, this is David and that's Ramsey," I say, introducing everyone, seeing as no one else has taken the initiative.

"Hey," he says, standing up straighter.

"So what are you doing here?" I ask, arms folded.

"Uhm," he mutters, appearing confused for a moment. "Didn't Ruby say?"

She giggles, the previous conversation seemingly forgotten. "They know you are here for me. I didn't get round to telling anyone yet that you are *here* right now."

"Ah," Cillian says. "Well...long story..."

"Just tell them," Ruby remarks, exasperated.

Already she is so comfortable with him. Is it because he

looks like Declan, it's easy to fall into familiarity with him, or is it so much deeper than that?

"Okay," he drawls. "Long story short...my boss told me to kill Ruby so that he could take over her operation in Manchester and I refused. That put me on the outs, so here I am, on the lam with you lot."

I raise an eyebrow. "And your boss is?" I ask.

He exchanges a glance with Declan. "Might as well get it out there," Declan says.

"Hm," Cillian murmurs.

"Wait!" David says. "Forget that for a minute. You're saying that Ruby's life is in danger and we're standing here on the side of the fucking road in plain sight for anyone to drive by?"

Man has a point. I position myself in front of Ruby, blocking her from view, but I turn back to Cillian.

"What's it going to take to get the hit off her head?" I ask.

He breathes out. "There is only one way and even that isn't a guarantee," he says. "And that's to take him out first."

I nod slowly, meeting Declan's gaze steadily before I look back at Cillian. The rest of the group is silent.

"And how do we go about doing that?" I ask.

"Pah," he scoffs. "Connor O'Leary is the most well protected man in Ireland, no one can get near him."

I frown. I know that name and it's not good. Not good at all.

"Unless we don't," Cillian adds quietly. "Get near him, that is. There is only one man in the entire world who will have a shot at him." He is staring directly at Declan.

We all turn to stare at the man, whose face has gone like stone.

"You want Declan to kill your boss?" David hisses, even though there is no one else around us for miles.

I shake my head. The difference is subtle to all but me, but

I'm starting to figure out how Declan's mind works. "No, not *kill*," I say and place my hand on Cillian's shoulder. "You have to put a hit out on the head of the Irish mafia."

Silence falls and all gazes land on Cillian.

Chapter Thirty

David

As one, we all turn our gazes to Cillian. He is pale. I don't blame him. Low-level killing within the mob is one thing, taking out the *head* is an entirely different ball game. I have to say that I'm marginally impressed that Cillian is so high up the food chain himself that he reports directly to the Alpha. Well, *was*, I suppose now.

No one says a word.

"So how do we decide if we're doing this?" I ask, taking the bull by the horns. "Whose decision is it? Ruby's, because it's her life? Cillian's, because he's paying? Declan, because he's the one who has to do it? All of us having a vote and majority wins? I don't know how this works."

Silence.

Ruby has her lips pursed and after a few seconds she pulls away from me, turning her back and walking over to stare out over the Atlantic Ocean, perhaps seeking guidance from her family across the way.

Cillian steps forward, but I stop him with a hand on his arm. "Leave her," I state.

He might be the big shot mafia dude, but when it comes to Ruby, *I'm* the expert. Even now, when she has changed slightly. A month ago, she would've dived in with gusto, making plans and getting off on the thrill of something so dangerous. Now, she is contemplating. She will come down on the side of yay for assassination, of that I have no doubt. She has been through the worst and come out of it. There is no way she wants to live in fear of her life being snuffed out. Not before, and especially not now.

"Ruby's choice," Cillian says eventually.

I shift my eyes to Declan. He is grim-faced and his whole demeanor has gone taut. I go to him and squeeze his hand. "You don't have to do it, if you don't want to," I whisper to him.

He turns his head to stare at me with that blank look. He blinks and then nods slowly. "It's not that," he says, shaking his head. "It's the aftermath."

"Yeah," I say and watch as Ramsey goes to Ruby. I knew he would. He's the one that can bring her back from the brink with this.

I lean forward on impulse and kiss Declan's forehead. He leans into it, closing his eyes and for one brief moment, he relaxes.

That is until Cillian splutters, and it tears us apart.

"Leave it," Declan mumbles to him and pulls away, going to Ruby as well.

I stare after him confused.

Turning back to Cillian, about to give him a speech on love is love and all that, I stop. His face is haunted and pale. I frown and bite my tongue. This isn't about a case of homophobia. This runs deeper into something pretty dark.

Declan said he had never been with another man before, but I'm starting to think that was a lie. He was too skilled to be a novice. It was too easy for him to take my dick in his mouth. My mouth goes dry, but I don't ask. If Declan wants to share, he can. It's not really any of my business if he has secrets that include sex with men. My only concern is if he is keeping secrets from Ruby. Could this potentially explode into a volatile situation? Declan is the master of his emotions. It's hard to tell some days if he even has any, but everyone has a breaking point. Judging by Cillian's face, this might just be his.

I clear my throat, turning Cillian's attention back to me after he also stared after Declan. He looks deep into my eyes, and I return the stare.

"You care about him?" he asks quietly as Layton, sensing something is up, also turns to go to Ruby, leaving us alone.

"Yes," I answer carefully.

"But you are in love with Ruby. I can see that much."

"I am."

He nods slowly. "If you hurt him or make him do anything he doesn't want to..." He takes a menacing step forward. "...I will make you wish you'd never been born."

I roll my eyes at him, surprising him. "Yeah, yeah," I drawl. "I'm more scared of him than you. Besides, you have nothing to worry about. There isn't a chance in hell *I* could make him do anything he doesn't want to."

Cillian snorts and gives me a once-over with a raised eyebrow. "Yeah, I see your point. Still, the promise stands."

"Noted," I say with narrowed eyes, offended by his assessment of me, but then I figure this isn't really about me. It's about Declan, so I let it go.

He gives me a smile, which I take as it was clearly meant, and return it.

"He is a remarkable man," I say.

"You have no idea," he says and then steps back when the rest of them rejoin us.

If my interest wasn't piqued before, it definitely is now.

The saying curiosity killed the cat echoes in my head.

But something tells me, this cat is going to have to dig a little deeper, to make sure that Ruby is protected at all costs.

"What is the verdict?" I ask, turning to Ruby.

"We decide on this together," she states. "Unanimous vote."

Chapter Thirty-One

Ruby

After it was agreed we would take the rest of the day to think about it, I climb back into the white sedan with Declan and Cillian. The rest of the men get back in the Range Rover. Declan pulls onto the road, and they follow.

"About ten minutes," Declan mutters.

I nod, about to close my eyes for a bit of a rest, my head is banging all of a sudden, when Cillian says, "Look, I know we just agreed not to talk about this with each other, but fuck that. It's just us here. Ruby, what are you thinking? Because I'm thinking this is a bad idea, but the only idea. And I get why *I* have to be the one to take out the hit, but this is going to put my arse in even bigger shite than it already is."

I sigh and turn to face him. "You don't have to worry about the fallout if we agree to go this route. I have a plan for you. Before we came here, I took out the head of one of the higher up gangs. Nasty man, nasty business, but I've decided to back *you* into taking his place and cleaning up the mess he's created. For example, I don't deal with drugs and prostitution. If you do, you don't anymore…"

He shakes his head.

"Good. So that's my plan for you."

He swallows and then launches himself at me through the seats and cups the back of my head to plant a kiss on me, filled with about half a dozen emotions, desire only one of them.

"Do you mind?" Declan grumbles. "You're in the bloody way."

Cillian pulls back with an elated smile. "You'd do that for me?"

"For *us*," I state. "It's mutually beneficial."

"Understood. I think I might just be falling in love with you, Ruby Bellingham."

"You wouldn't be the first one," Declan mutters, making me blush.

Cillian sits back and then a few minutes later, he groans, "Oh, you have got to be kidding me."

"What?" I ask and look out of the side window where Declan has pulled up in front of a small cottage.

"Didn't have a choice," Declan says and gets out quickly.

I frown and see him go over to a gorgeous redhead that is…*as thin as a fucking rail*.

"Siobhan!" I roar and shove the car door open so hard with my foot, it bounces back and bangs me on the knee. "Oww, you fucker. And you!" I snarl, marching up to Declan once I've hobbled up the pathway.

"She can help," he says and then brushes past her to enter the cottage.

"Hi," she says, holding her hand up in an awkward wave. "I'm Siobhan."

"Yeah, I know," I grit out. "Ruby."

"Yep," she says and then looks over my shoulder. "Nice to see you again, Cillian."

"Humph," he mutters and hangs back, looking shifty.

I grimace at him and also brush past Siobhan to enter the house and end up directly in the kitchen. Cillian trails reluctantly in after me, with Siobhan bringing up the rear and closing the door. I glance out of the window and see the Range Rover pull up.

"How can she help?" I ask Declan, being really rude.

"At some point we need to head home. With that in mind, Cillian's cover identity will be flagged wherever Connor has people, which I'm guessing is everywhere. He needs a new passport and Siobhan can give it to him."

"Oh," I say, feeling a little bit, just a tiny bit, abashed. "Guess she can help, then."

He rolls his eyes at me, and then says, "Cillian, join me outside for a minute."

I curse the day they were born when they abandon me with their ex.

I turn back to her with a stiff smile. "So..."

She laughs. "I'm not the wicked witch of the west, you know," she says. "You don't have to worry about me. I am curious though," she says, turning to put the kettle on. "How did you manage to do what I couldn't?"

"What's that then?" I ask warily.

"Get both of them to be with you at the same time," she states bluntly.

"Oh, uhm," I stammer, suddenly shy.

"I'm not an eejit. I can see with my own two eyes how they're both looking at you," she says with a laugh.

"Well, uhm, Declan and I have been...involved for some time. It's complicated and Cillian is...new," I explain.

"I see," she says, nodding sagely as if that all made sense. "You are a lucky girl. I tried for years, but it wasn't happening. I eventually cut ties and now I'm happily married." She holds up her left hand to show me her ring.

It eases my discomfort of being here with her a tiny bit.

"Oh, lovely," I murmur.

"You aren't going to ask?" she says with a smirk.

"Ask what?"

"If I found another set of twins to live out my fantasy."

I blink. "Did you?" I ask.

She snorts. "Yes."

"And you married both of them?"

She nods. "Not exactly commonplace 'round these parts."

"Or any parts," I giggle, feeling more at ease with her as the seconds go by.

"Fact," she says. "But who gives a shite, right?"

"Right," I say with a genuine smile now.

She hands me a cup of tea and then looks out of the window. "Who are they?" she asks, indicating Layton, Ramsey and David.

"Oh, they are also with me," I say, proudly, almost smugly.

Her eyes go wide as she turns back to me. "Go and shite," she says. "Five of them? And here I thought I was the dog's bollocks with my two." She laughs so hard, she spills her tea. "How is that?" Her green eyes search mine interestedly.

"Amazing," I say. "Although, like I said, Cillian is new."

She nods and doesn't push for details, thankfully.

"Can I ask you something?" I say, going over all brave.

"Of course." She props herself up against the counter, settling in for a good gossip by the looks of it.

"How come Mary Gannon knows about you and Declan but not you and Cillian? Especially seeing as you got married?" I ask, taking a stab in the dark with my assessment of this situation.

"Ah," she says. "Well, Cillian pulled away from his family after he moved out. All the shite with their da, it really affected him. I met him then and never met his mam or sister. I only met Declan by chance one day…I saw him on Grafton Street and thought he was Cillian!" she says. "Anyway, after a while Cillian made it clear it wasn't going to happen with the three of us, so I jumped ship and ended up landing on Declan's... deck, if you get my meaning." She gives me a sassy wink. "He was difficult, and it didn't last long. I knew then I wanted to get back with Cillian and we got married, but by then what we'd had before fizzled and I asked for a divorce not long after. They never said any of this?"

"I didn't ask," I mutter, embarrassed.

"Oh, ha," she comments. "I get you. It was all a long time ago. Ancient history." She shrugs and I take her at her word.

"You know about their past?" I ask quietly, hating myself for the fish. I should be asking them, not her.

She shrugs. "Some, not all. Cillian is more of an open book about it than Declan is. It's like getting blood from a stone with that one. Behind those blue eyes lies a deep trauma that blackened his soul."

"Yeah," I mutter, really hoping that Declan didn't share his deep trauma with Scar. Something tells me that with alcohol or not, if he didn't tell Siobhan, he wouldn't have told my sister. But Siobhan has unwittingly given me some valuable information. If Declan doesn't spill, Cillian will.

"Anyway, I'd better get on. You'll be wanting that passport soon," she says, finishing her tea and placing the cup in the sink.

I nod. "How did you get into this?" I ask a question about her, so it doesn't sound like I was only pumping her for information on the Gannon twins. Not that I was, or anything...

"Where we grew up, so many kids ended up in the gangs when they didn't want to be. I saw the destruction it caused to families. I wanted to help. This is my way of helping anyone who wants out to escape."

"You're doing a good thing," I murmur, knowing how some bosses are of the mind that it's 'in for life'.

"Yeah," she says with a smile and disappears into a back room, leaving me to stare out at the men embroiled in a discussion that looks serious and doesn't involve me.

I don't like the look of this one bit. I sense a ganging-up about to happen and I don't mean that in the good sense either.

Fuckers.

Chapter Thirty-Two

Ramsey

Ruby is glaring at us as we enter the cottage, both Layton and I ducking our heads to get through the small doorway. She knows we've been up to something, and she is pissed. She's about to get even more angry when she hears what we have to say.

"Well?" she hisses. "What have you been plotting behind my back?"

"Not so much behind your back," I start, having been given the perilous task of confronting her with this, on the assumption that she won't blow up as much at me than anyone else. I argued that David was more likely to be well-received, but he point blank refused, so here we are.

"Oh?" she snarls.

If I was concerned about her having a fragile state of mind, I am no longer. She is blazing with the fires of hell right now. I almost chicken out.

"We have come to an agreement about what to do about this Connor situation," I say, after clearing my throat. "As a group. We will still vote, but ours counts as one on this because we are completely in agreement about what should be done and why."

"Are you now?" she drawls, fury simmering in the green depths of her eyes. "And do, pray tell, what you are in agreement about."

I gulp. She went all schoolmarm on me, and it sent me right back to being called into the Headmistresses office in high school.

"We have agreed that Connor needs taking out," I state, folding my arms defensively, as if that is going to stop the blasting I'm about to get.

Weirdly, it doesn't happen.

She falls back a step, and her face goes blank. "I see," she says. "And your vote outweighs mine, is that it?"

"No," I say, going to her. "That's not what we're doing here. We are scared to death about losing you, and we think..." I look back over my shoulder nervously. At Declan's encouraging nod, I turn back to her. "We think that you are going to decide not to go through with it," I rush out.

"What makes you think that?" she asks slowly.

Luckily, David answers that. "A few weeks ago, you would have ordered the hit and we'd be on our way to get it done. You hesitated, which means the game has changed. It's okay to be scared, Rubes. You've been through a lot and getting back on the horse will take time. We are just trying to help you make the right decision."

"Think you know me so well?" she asks quietly.

It's like a kick in the nuts.

"My hesitation has *nothing* to do with being scared of making the decision. My hesitation, my need to think this through is because if we do this, we are declaring war. A war that I'm not sure I'm strong enough to fight just yet when my turf is currently not exactly in my hands. This has *nothing* to do with being scared," she reiterates harshly. "I'm being cautious, trying to make sure that we can do this and survive. They will come at us from all sides and if you think we are prepared for that, then by all means, whack him right now."

She gives us all a filthy look and then marches off into the cottage, where none of us dare to follow her.

"I *knew* this was a bad fucking idea!" I spit out.

"No, it was the *right* idea," David says. "If we hadn't gone at her from that angle, we'd still be in the dark about what she's thinking. It was devious, but now we know. We have to get back home where she feels stronger. We need to leave here tomorrow at the latest."

"And what about the police?" I ask. "They aren't just going to stop looking for her overnight."

"I know,' David says. "But I may have a way around that if I call in a bunch of favors. I just need to make a few phone calls."

"This is bad, so bad," I mutter and then abandon the men to go after Ruby.

I find her in a small room off the short hallway. "Sorry," I murmur, getting that out there before anything else.

"It's fine," she huffs. "I get it. I do. You all think that I'm still the broken little doll that I was when I stumbled out of that room a few weeks ago. But I'm not. Okay, yes, I'm being more cautious than usual, but that is because of all of you. If I ordered this to be done and lost one or more of you...I couldn't bear it. Do you understand that?"

"Yes," I say and take her in my arms.

She turns in my embrace and sighs when she wraps her arms around me. "How come you drew the short straw?" she asks wearily.

I snicker. "They seemed to think you wouldn't kill me as quickly as the others."

"They'd be right," she says with a laugh and then tilts her head back, reaching up to cup my face.

I feel like I've won the lottery.

I take the risk and bend down to kiss her. She clings to me, fisting her hands in my t-shirt. I push my tongue against hers. She thrusts hers back, moving her hand around to the back of my neck to pull me closer to her. She kisses me in a way that is so sexy, making me imagine all the things she could do with her tongue. I stop thinking. I run my hands up her back, under her t-shirt and she freezes.

It takes me a second to register, and then I groan and pull back, removing my hands.

"I'm sorry," I mutter, disappointment, regret, sorrow coursing through me.

"No," she says, taking my hands and placing them on her hips. "If I don't do this, I will have failed as your girlfriend and I detest failure," she says, a small smile playing on her lips.

"Girlfriend," I whisper and slip my hands back under her top, but take it slow and steady so she can get used to feeling them there. "I like the sound of that."

"That's what we agreed on," she reminds me.

"I know. I guess with all the others, I thought it would be redefined." I am fucking elated. I want to sing and dance and shout it from the rooftops for all of the world to hear.

She shakes her head. "No. I don't see it that way."

"Good," I whisper against her mouth. "I love you."

"I love you," she says, which fills my heart with joy.

I kiss her again, feeling her press her body against mine. I want to ravage her. I want to lift her up onto the windowsill and fuck her until she screams my name, but that isn't going to happen. I will take what she is offering me and if she wants to take it further, she can.

Chapter Thirty-Three

Ruby

After we have settled into the safehouse, a few miles down the road from Siobhan's, I find myself alone and in desperate need of it. I've been given the master bedroom in this cottage, which is furnished quite lavishly for something that may never get used. Not that I'm complaining. I like lavish things.

The time has come for some things to be done. I reach for the hem of my tee and pull it over my head. I drop it on the armchair and toe off my sneakers before I take off my sweats. I pull the soft, stretchy bra over my head and discard my panties. Naked, I walk into the en-suite bathroom and close the door quietly. Inhaling deeply, I turn to the mirror and look at myself properly for the first time since before I was taken.

I blink and run my fingertips over the very faint scar across my throat. This is the first time I've looked at it, let alone touched it. I swallow and lower my hand quickly.

Breathing deeply, I then press my fingertips to the scar on my stomach before I drop my eyes to look at it. It is all healed up, but still tender and pink. I prod it carefully, but it doesn't make me flinch as I suspected it would. Michelle did a good job of patching me up, and Declan removed the bandage when it was time. I drop my hand lower to the bullet graze scar on my thigh, feeling that. Getting to know it.

I unzip my toiletry bag, which is waiting for me on the counter. I pull out the tube of sensitive hair remover and set to work on the bush that has sprouted between my legs over the last month. It has been a long, long time since I had pubic hair and I *don't* like it. I leave the cream to set and then grab the tweezers. I lean forward and start plucking my eyebrows into some order, wondering how in the hell these men still love me. I am a mess. Emotionally, physically, mentally. Christ.

Once my eyebrows are done, I reach in the bag for a claw clip and twirl my hair up, securing it tightly and then set about shaving my armpits.

Once the time is up on the hair remover, I scrape it off and grimace, then grab the waxing strips to finish it off.

I brace myself for the pain, but it's actually not that bad anymore. Once you've been stabbed in the gut, you redefine your pain threshold by a lot.

Happy with the job I've done, but left with no doubt that a professional needs to get down there really soon, I turn towards the shower and turn the taps on. Grabbing the razor, I lather up my legs and shave away the stubble before I climb in fully and carefully wash every inch of myself, except my hair.

This methodical, almost ritualistic cleansing soothes my nerves and when I step out of the shower, I feel more at ease. I apply a thin layer of softly scented body lotion on my arms and legs and across my stomach before I face myself again.

"Better, Rubes. Much, much better."

I unclip my hair and watch as it tumbles down around my shoulders. I brush it out and then draw in a deep breath.

I'm ready.

I push open the bathroom door and check the clock. Layton said he would come and check on me in forty-five minutes and time is up.

I arrange myself on the bed as there is a soft knock at the bedroom door.

My stomach twists into a knot.

I'm ready.

"Come in," I call out softly and the door opens.

"Everything okay? Oh, fuck, oh, I...uhm..." he stammers when he sees me naked on the bed and turns around to leave.

"Wait," I say, stopping him. "Look at me."

He pauses, his back turned towards me. He is the size of the doorway, dressed in a tight black t-shirt and black combat pants. He is sexy as fuck. I focus on that and not on anything else. He slowly turns, those bright blue eyes of his, sweeping over me before he meets my eyes.

Yes.

I breathe out in relief. It's working. His gaze on me, so full of lust and longing is exactly what I needed to see.

"Get the others," I whisper. "Please."

"Ruby..."

"Please, Layton. I know what I'm doing."

And I do.

After abstaining for a couple of years last time, I finally figured I was ready to get back on the horse, so to speak. It was fine. Derek was capable and he didn't make me feel threatened in any way. I didn't love him, but I was ready.

Now, after only a few weeks. I know I can do this. I can move past the horror and get back the life that was cruelly taken away from me. Or maybe it wasn't cruel. Maybe I deserved it.

Whatever.

All I know now is that I need to do this. For me. For them. For the men I love.

"Please," I say steadily. "Go and get the other men."

He nods slowly and backs out, closing the door quietly.

I sit in contemplation *knowing* that they are having a massive discussion about this downstairs. I tap my fingers, wishing they'd hurry up so we can start whatever it is I plan on doing with them once they are all here. The waiting is the worst part. Sitting here like an idiot while they flap their tongues like a bunch of old women.

I'm about to get up and demand that they all hurry the fuck up and get in here, when I hear the footsteps on the stairs.

My heart skips a beat, but I'm okay.

I wait as the door opens again and Declan, leading the charge, storms in and throws a blanket over me, dousing whatever arousal had been simmering.

"No," he says, defiantly. "Just no."

"Excuse me?" I choke out, shoving the blanket off me. "No, what?"

"Don't do this. You don't need to do this. We will wait."

"Easy for you to say," I retort, all guns blazing. "You got some earlier."

David snorts loudly. "Well, she's not wrong there, Irish."

Then he looks at Cillian, who is looking everywhere except at me. "Does that make you Irish Two? Nah, never mind, I'll find a name for you."

"Hello?" I shout out, waving my hand about. "I'm naked here. Doesn't *anyone* want me? You're about to give me a massive complex."

"I want you," Layton says, quite bravely seeing as Declan throws him a look that would quite easily take the place of his sniper rifle on any given day. "Do you want me, sweetheart?" he asks, ignoring Declan and approaching the bed, and me, like a panther stalking its prey.

I know he is doing this on purpose. He expects me to pull

the blanket up and tell them all to get fucked (not by me) and get out. But his little plan backfires. I rise to my knees, hearing all of their breath deepen at the sight of me.

"Yes," I purr, the thrill of this game, the high from the control I have over this situation, spurring me on. I know this is right, and I'm ready. "Come and get me."

Chapter Thirty-Four

Layton

She's the devil.

Well and truly.

Not to mention, the strongest woman I have ever met.

She knows what she wants, and she is taking her life back regardless of any fucker who tried to take it.

"I love you so much, sweetheart," I murmur. "I'm going to ask you this once and only once. I will accept whatever answer you give me. Are you sure you are ready for this?"

"Yes," she says immediately, with no hesitation whatsoever. "On one condition."

I hold back and wait.

"This is going to go *my* way. You know I need the play, but not today. I just want this to be about us. Can you do that?"

"Yes," I reply without hesitation. I can do vanilla sex. I think. I used to do it all the time before the darkness of being a sniper in the Armed Forces enveloped me and I needed that outlet to serve my demons.

"All of you?" she asks.

After verbal confirmation, I pull off my tee and chuck it on the armchair in the corner. I give her time to take in the fact that I'm half naked and not going anywhere near her. She licks her lips, making my cock go hard.

But then her eyes flick to Cillian, who has practically squashed himself into the corner of the room.

"Come here," she says, holding out her hand.

"I'll just watch, see where I fit in," he croaks out.

She giggles. "No, that's not how it works," she says gently.

"Errr," he stammers.

"Oh, for feck's sake, man. She wants you. Why are you still standing there?" Declan snaps at him.

I watch with amusement as he comes closer, and she smiles smugly, but turns her attention back to me. She walks on her knees over to the edge of the bed and I move closer to her. She reaches out to undo my pants slowly. I watch her, waiting to see if she will bolt but she doesn't. She pulls my cock out and with determination, she bends down to take it in her mouth. I want to stop her, but as soon as her lips close over my tip, I'm lost to her filthy mouth.

"Fuck," I groan, "Ruby." I shove my hand into her hair.

Sliding her tongue down my extensive length, I close my eyes and drop my head back, enjoying the sensation immensely.

"Oh, that's hot," David murmurs.

"Have you got your phone?" I ask, opening my eyes and looking over at him.

He nods warily.

"Record this. I want her to watch it back while she rubs her clit and makes herself come."

"Uhn," she moans, her mouth full of my cock.

"She said..." David starts.

"This isn't for now. It's for later," I assure him.

"Ruby?" he asks.

She nods her head, still giving me the best blow job I've ever received. Her hot mouth is driving me wild. I want to take over and fuck her mouth harshly, but she laid down the rules and I have to let her go at her own pace.

Satisfied that David is doing as I ask, I close my eyes again. Ruby grazes her teeth over my tip, and I let out a soft groan. I pull away, needing to see to her now.

"Are you ready for me, sweetheart?" I ask quietly.

She nods and lies back, her legs clamped together. I run my hands lightly up her shins, over her thighs and up to her hips.

"Open up for me," I murmur.

She does.

Slowly.

I breathe in deeply when I catch sight of her glistening clit and bend down to lick her all the way up her slit.

She hisses, her thighs going taut, but I don't stop. If she says the words, I will without hesitation. Her body is trembling, and it brings Ramsey over to her.

"We don't need to do this," he says desperately.

"Yes, we do," she whispers. "Keep going."

I try not to take offense at that. She's made it sound clinical, but I *do* get it. I knew the first time like this would be difficult for her. It's why I'm going slow and trying to arouse her. If I had my way, I'd be fucking her senseless already.

She gives me a shaky smile and I take it as it was dealt. I press my mouth to her clit and suck it gently into my mouth, something I know will get her going. I'm not wrong. She bucks on the bed and dampens my mouth with the spike in her arousal. I smile and tug on her before I let her go and thrust my tongue into her pussy. She cries out and reaches for

Ramsey. He is there for her, on the bed and grips her hand, lacing their fingers together. His expression is one of pain that she's going through this, but I have to keep going. She singled me out to do this. Declan might've been the one to take the initial step with her and I understand why. It's his role with her. But this time all together, she trusts me to handle this correctly. It's clear Ramsey would've stopped, and David probably wouldn't have even started.

I taste her juices on my tongue and groan softly. I grip her thighs hard enough to keep hold of her, but not hard enough to restrain her. She needs to know she can get up and leave at any second.

"Ruby," I pant, feeling my dick aching. "Can I take you?"

"Yes," she says. "Yes."

It's all I need. I drag her down the bed and position my cock at her entrance. With my eyes on hers, I thrust once, deep enough to fill her completely. She gasps at the invasion, but then she quivers, her nipples peaking. I pull back slightly and thrust again, finding a rhythm she is comfortable with.

"Fuck, yes," I groan, so grateful that I'm inside her and she's enjoying it. "Is that good, sweetheart?"

"Yes!" she cries out. "So good. Fuck me harder, Layton, please don't hold back."

At her words, I growl and grip her hips tightly. I pound into her, my ten-inch cock riding her pussy with everything I've got.

"I love you, Ruby. Fuck, I love you," I rasp and then she arches her back, her climax hitting her hard.

I grunt in relief that I made her come; it wasn't a given.

She moans and writhes on the bed. Ramsey is watching her with desire hooding his eyes.

I let myself explode inside her, flooding her with my cum and marking her as mine. One last thrust and I drain myself dry, panting furiously. I pull out, my cock dripping with our cum and let her go to Ramsey, happy with the knowledge that I did right by her and that she has moved forward for however long it lasts, and if the day comes where she regresses, we will start all over again, taking care of her one day at a time. For now, she is at peace.

Chapter Thirty-Five

Ruby

I crawl into Ramsey's lap, struggling to get his pants undone. Now that Layton has taken care of the 'first time', I feel more at ease. I realized about halfway through, that what Smith did to me wasn't about sex. It was about power. He had it, I didn't. The sex is neither here nor there in the grand scheme of things. The power, though? *That* is bigger, greater, and I have it back. I have five men in this room who would do anything for me, anything I ask. If that isn't power, then I don't know what is.

I feel like a goddess and finally, *finally*, feel like myself again. I stroke Ramsey's huge cock, enjoying the feel of it in my hand. I jerk him off steadily, needing to keep moving. Always moving now. I was immobile at the hands of Boomer and Smith. No power.

I shake the thoughts from my mind and focus on the big dick that I need inside me. The more dicks the better to erase Smith's puny prick. I think I've gone slightly mad. The thoughts are racing, but I have to keep moving.

I slide down on Ramsey, taking in his entire length before I settle and start to ride him, slowly, rotating my hips. "David," I pant. "Come to me."

He does, straight away.

Power.

"Touch me."

He groans softly, coming up behind me and cupping my breasts. He tweaks my nipples gently until I moan, and then he twists them roughly.

"Yes," I cry out, feeling myself get wetter.

David kisses my neck. Ramsey leans forward to kiss my mouth. I'm caught between the two, but I'm not trapped. In order to prove that to myself and them, I wiggle out from in between them and turn to face David. He is naked and delicious. I run my hands down his chest, bending down to take his cock in my mouth. He shoves his hand into my hair to hold me close but not control me. Ramsey shuffles onto his knees and then rams into me from behind, unable to help the passion, the drive to fuck me hard and fast.

I groan, the vibration causing David to pant. I suck him a bit more, but then he pulls away. Ramsey slams into me, his breathing ragged. My climax is building. I want it. I need it. It hits me hard, and I cry out, my pussy clenching around Ramsey's cock, milking him until he releases inside me, shooting his load and filling me up.

"Yes, baby," I rasp. "Yes."

David wastes no time in replacing Ramsey behind me, but instead he pulls me back so that I'm straddling him, reverse-cowgirl.

Declan, practically flies across the bed and attaches his mouth to my clit, tugging on it while David's cock stretches my pussy wide.

Power.

I have it. They don't.

That thought alone, has my pussy soaking David's cock even more. He almost whimpers as I start to ride him, with Declan's mouth keeping up, licking and flicking my clit until I explode in a display of fireworks as the blood rushes through my body. I convulse, once, twice, my pussy tightens its hold on David's cock until I hear him cry out in triumph. He comes, panting heavily, his hands on my tits.

"Rubes," he murmurs, turning my head and kissing me. "I love you."

"Love you," I murmur and then, I'm yanked from David's cock to fall onto Declan who is flat on his back, an expression on his face of adoration and awe.

"You are perfect," he murmurs. "Just perfect."

My heart swells with love for him, for all of them. Then the wicked thought enters my head, and I can't help it.

Declan sees it and chuckles. "Only for you, Princess," he murmurs.

Like a woman whose birthdays and Christmases have come all at once, I hold my hand out to Cillian.

His eyes go wide, and his mouth drops open.

Oh, the power has me practically creaming myself.

"How?" he asks warily.

"One in the front, one in the back," David pipes up, "and for the love of God, let me watch."

"Still recording?" I ask, because for the love of God and everything downstairs as well. I *need* to watch this myself.

"Yep," he says and indicates the phone he propped up on the dresser.

I snicker. "Do not ever lose that fucking thing, do you hear me?"

"Oh, way ahead of you," he says, laughing. "You think I want my knob plastered all over the internet? Yeah, nope."

I can't help the burst of laughter. It is exactly what I needed at the exact right time.

"Come," I murmur to Cillian. "Have you done anal before?"

He splutters and chokes while Declan stifles his amusement with a badly disguised cough.

"Okay, swap," I say.

Declan and I rearrange ourselves.

"You really need to up your sex game," Layton says to Cillian, laying on the end of the bed and watching us with hooded eyes.

"No fecking kidding," he mutters and strips off with all eyes on him.

I can't help but glance down. Yep, same size as Declan. Fuck. Me.

I cannot wait to watch this later, but right now, I inhale deeply as Declan starts to lube up my rear hole with some Vaseline lip balm that Ramsey handed him from the dresser.

"It'll do," he murmurs, running his hand over the puckered hole before slipping the tip of his finger inside.

I grunt.

It's been a while.

I figured at some point this would happen. Four men, now five, aren't going to line up to fuck me one by one forever.

"Oh, mmm," I groan, closing my eyes as Declan stretches my hole, readying me for his cock.

"Jaysus," Cillian mutters, climbing onto the bed, cock stiff and so ready for me.

I lick my lips, dying to take them both.

Eventually, Declan mutters that I'm ready and sits back. I wiggle backwards, sitting on him, face forward. I lean back and lift my hips.

"Can I?" David whispers to Declan.

"Yes," he replies.

I see the shock in Cillian's eyes, the way he completely freezes up when David takes hold of Declan's cock and guides it to the entrance of my back passage. I push down, gasping as his huge dick squeezes into the small hole.

"Oh, my God," I groan, throwing my head back.

"Fucking hell," David mutters. "Oh, fuck." He starts to jerk off at the sight of Declan's cock in my ass.

"Cillian," I purr. "Come to me. You can do this, I need you, okay?"

"Yes," he murmurs and kneels in front of me.

With David jerking off on one side of me, and Ramsey taking his cock in his hand on the other, and Layton watching from the edge of the bed, Cillian takes his dick and presses it against my clit, rotating slowly.

"Fuck," I pant, riding Declan's cock. "Fuck, fuck, yes."

Cillian starts to get into it, rubbing the head of his cock over my clit, harder and faster. I come in a sudden rush of blood straight to my pussy, and then I squirt, spraying juice all over Cillian's cock.

"Fucking hell, love," he pants. "That is the sexiest thing I've ever seen."

I give him a sassy smile, my pussy still clenching wildly and then he enters me. He pushes his cock deep inside me.

"Hot, so fucking hot," David rasps. He leans forward to kiss me, cupping the back of my head and plunging his tongue into my mouth quickly before pulling away again.

"Mmm," I moan as the feelings start to overwhelm me. I scrunch my eyes shut, feeling the air rush out of my lungs.

It's too much, too much.

Moaning, I open my eyes again, ready to remove myself from this situation, but Cillian's deep blue eyes are on mine, full of love and desire and it calms me instantly.

"That's it, baby," I pant. "Ride me hard."

He thrusts furiously, driving his cock deeper inside me. The orgasm that starts to build comes from my toes first, all the way up my body. I tremble in between the twins, my eyes wide, my mouth open in a silent scream of ecstasy as I shudder violently on their dicks, coming intensely like I never have before.

I scream out loud when Layton appears in the place of David and starts to rub my clit, needing to touch me.

"Fuck, yes!" I roar, feeling another orgasm build up and crash over the edge of the cliff, taking me with it in its wave of hedonistic frenzy as the twins pound me from both ends. Declan finishes first, groaning loudly as he comes in my ass and Cillian follows soon after, unloading in my pussy, filling me with cum.

"Ruby," he pants. "Ruby…"

He leans forward to kiss me, tangling his fingers in my hair. I kiss him back, desperately, still impaled on the twin's cocks as Layton continues to tease my clit until I squirt again all over his hand with a loud cry, muffled by Cillian's mouth.

"There you go, sweetheart. That is fucking sexy."

Power.

It's all about the power.

I have it. I have it all.

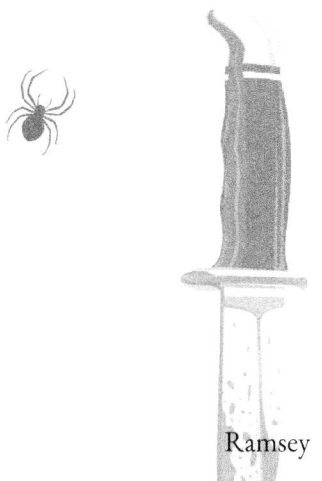

Chapter Thirty-Six

Ramsey

I haven't left her side since she fell asleep. I don't want to. I can't. She looks so vulnerable, yet she seems to be at peace. At least she is resting for now.

I look up when the door opens quietly and Layton gestures for me to follow him. Climbing off the bed carefully, I do up my pants, still undone from when we fucked and quietly leave the room, shutting the door behind me.

"What's up?" I ask when I see the other four men gathered in the hallway outside the bedroom.

"We've got bad news," Layton says.

"You get to tell Ruby," David adds hastily.

I groan. "Again? Why me? I took the bullet last time."

"You know why," Declan says.

"Why can't Cillian do it? He's new. He should learn. Baptism by fire," I complain.

"Pass," Cillian says. "Don't you even want to know what the bad news is?"

"Yes," I grumble. "Go on."

Layton's face goes dark when he says, "Cillian has a source who has just informed him that Connor is on his way to Manchester. We have to go back and let Declan take him out."

"Jesus," I mutter. This is the last thing that Ruby needs. "What about the police sniffing around?"

"I have managed to divert their attention in a different direction," David says cagily. "I owe some very scary people, big time."

"Which direction?" I grit out.

"Hmm, the less you know the better," he mutters.

"Great," I say. "Just great."

"So, go on then," Declan says, more anxious than I have ever seen him.

"Give me a minute," I hiss. "Not only do I have to go in there and wake her up, but I also have to…"

"AAAAH! AAAAH! No! Boomer, please don't let him do this!"

As one, we turn to the bedroom door where Ruby is shouting. I lunge for it, yanking it open and fighting Layton for who gets to go in first. Turns out, I win and rush to the bed, where Ruby is sitting up, holding the sides of her head and shaking it violently.

"Ruby," I say, taking her hands. "Look at me. You're safe. Look at me."

Her wild eyes come up to meet mine and my heart breaks for her. She is terrified.

"You're safe," I say again, but don't pull her towards me. I just let her hear my words.

She blinks, the fear turning to nothing in her eyes. Absolutely dead. It scares me how she is able to do that. Just switch off like that.

"Yeah," she says. "They're both dead."

She pulls her hands from mine and drags the sheet up to

cover her bare breasts. I hadn't even noticed. I step back, giving her room.

"What's wrong?" she asks suddenly. "How did you all get in here so quickly?"

"We were lurking," David says. "Ramsey has some news."

Her gaze flicks to mine, a simmering anger now filling those pools of green delight. "Oh?" she bites out.

I turn and give the other four men a look that would kill.

"Why the daggers?" she asks. "What don't you want to tell me? And why you again? These four a bunch of pussys?"

The splutter of indignation makes me laugh. She gives me a smirk, which is in total contrast to the state she woke up from.

"Yes," I state firmly. "They are. Look, Rubes. I'm just going to come out and say this. Connor is on his way to England, and we need a decision on what we're going to do about him."

Her eyes narrow. "Why?"

"Uhm. Why what?"

"Why has he gone to England?" She shoots her gaze over to Cillian.

"Remember Tadgh?" he asks her.

She nods slowly. "Well, he still has his in. He rang and said Connor is on his way to Manchester to take your operation. He is hoping to draw you out."

"Jesus," she mutters. "We can't go back…I'm in serious shit."

"Not anymore," I reassure her before David can and apparently steal this thunder.

"Hey!" he spits out. "My news. Not yours."

"You tasked me to tell Ruby the news, without my consent. I get to take credit for whatever the fuck I want…"

"Boys, stop," she says, holding her hand to her head. "Cillian. Do you still trust Tadgh?"

"Yeah. He's got my back."

"So, we go. Simple," she says.

"And?" Declan asks quietly.

"We go to war," she says absently, climbing out of bed, dragging the sheet with her to wrap around herself. She silently picks up her handbag and digs through it until she pulls out her purse. She opens it and has a poke through. We all watch as she removes a twenty Pound note and hands it to Declan.

"It's all I've got. Will it do for a deposit?" she asks.

"For what?" he asks, his tone icy.

"To take out Connor O'Leary before he can ruin everything I've worked for and potentially kill me first," she says matter-of-factly.

"We agreed Cillian would be the one to take out the hit," Layton says carefully.

"I didn't agree to anything," she says. "And why should he get the glory? My business, my life, my decision."

Declan snatches it out of her hand and my mouth goes dry.

"It'll do," he says. "But I expect the rest of my fee before I execute."

Eyes wide, I glare at him. "What the fuck, man?" I ask.

"Agreed," she says. "How much is it?" she adds, scrunching up her nose.

"Hundred kay," he says. "Although, it should be said, that is discounted. Mate's rates."

"Fuck you," she says, shaking her head with a smile. "You know I'm good for the full amount."

Now I'm dying to know how much he actually charges to kill someone. I wonder if he would tell me if I asked.

"So is that it then?" I ask. "Are we sorted?"

"We are. How soon will Siobhan be with Cillian's new passport?"

"I've already asked her to rush it. A couple of hours."

She nods, her face grim. "Guess, we're going home today, after all."

"He's going to have a few hours head start," I say, pointing out the obvious to everyone's annoyance, but fuck that. It needed to be said out loud.

"Yep," she says and then disappears into the bathroom, closing the door on us and then we hear the shower.

"Not it next time," I say, getting that out there.

"Let's leave her to process," Declan says. "Besides, Tadgh is on his way here. He has more information to tell us that might give us the upper hand."

I glance at the bathroom door, but follow the rest of the men out of the bedroom, hoping that when we get home, Ruby doesn't crumble because it's clear that no matter how much of a strong front she is putting on, she is still deeply traumatized by what happened to her. It's going to be a long, hard road and I feel this is only going to make it worse.

Chapter Thirty-Seven

Ruby

Making my way downstairs, after showering away great sex and packing my bag to leave in a hurry – yet again, I contemplate on something I did, or rather didn't do, with Cillian. We have never had the "do I need to use protection" talk. I mean with four other guys in the room going bareback, one would assume that we are all fine with it. I should have said something, but to be honest, Declan's previous comment about his twin not being with anyone since Siobhan stuck with me, so I'm sure he is all squared away. Assuming, of course, Declan knows that for a fact.

Anyway, what's done is done. I doubt Cillian would have knowingly gone into it if he knew he shouldn't have. He doesn't strike me as the type to be an insensitive asshole.

"Hey," I say when I see them all gathered in the front room. "We ready to go?"

"Tadgh isn't here yet," Cillian says worriedly, but then

turns as a car crunches on the gravel outside. He peeks around the drawn curtain and relaxes. "He's here now."

I tense up. I can't help it. Acting on pure instinct, I cross over to Declan and wrap my arms around him. He smiles down at me and kisses me swiftly, but I grab his head and deepen the kiss until I can hear that Tadgh has entered the room. Nothing wrong with showing him that I do in fact belong to Declan, in a manner of speaking, of course.

I hear a grunt and satisfied that my point has been made, I pull back. Declan is giving me a curious look, but I ignore him and cuddle into him, placing my head on his shoulder.

I don't know what it is about that giant psycho that strikes fear into my soul, but fuck if it isn't real.

"Are you okay?" Declan whispers in my ear.

"Mm-hm," I murmur. "Just fine."

He kisses the top of my head and then untangles himself from me to cross over to Cillian. They have a quiet talk with Tadgh, who seemingly can't resist shooting me a glance over the tops of their heads.

"Seriously?" Cillian spits out all of a sudden. "That fuck."

"What is it?" I ask, going over to them.

"He has already ordered the hit on you," Declan says. "But don't worry about it, we've got this."

I nod slowly, my blood running cooler. It's just any other day at the office. I thrive on the darkness and the thrill of this world and now I have to embrace that and push the slight smidge of fear aside.

"What else?" I ask.

"He's taken four men with him. Highest ranking members of the mafia," Tadgh says, his black eyes focusing on mine.

I blink. "Really?" I ask with a raised eyebrow.

"What are you thinking?" Declan asks with a frown.

"Full sweep," I say. "You up for it?"

He balks slightly.

Cillian chokes back a cough.

Tadgh grunts his approval.

"Why not?" Declan says, recovering quickly. "If you are absolutely sure."

"I am. And to be honest, I want him to know I'm coming."

"Ruby, no," Declan says, taking my arm and squeezing it. "You are not going anywhere near them."

"Yeah, I am. I'm not sitting back and letting you have all the fun. It's been a while since I got my hands dirty. I want to scrub blood out from under my fingernails. I want…"

He cuts me off by pressing his lips to mine. "You don't have anything to prove," he murmurs.

"I do. To myself. I will leave the four protection detail to you, *I* want to take out Connor myself."

"Don't be a fool," Tadgh growls at me. "He will shoot you as soon as he sees you coming."

"Then he won't see me coming. Or he will, but it will be through the haze of blood pouring out of his eyes."

"Jaysus," Cillian mutters. "Savage, aren't you, love?"

"Like it?" I challenge him.

"Fuck, yes," he breathes like a fool.

I smirk and clap my hands. "It's settled then. When do we go?"

"As soon as Siobhan gets here," Declan says, pursing his sexy lips.

I know he wants to protect me from all the big bad things of the world, but he seems to forget that *I'm* one of them. This mission is exactly what I need to feel like myself again and I'll be damned if I let anyone stand in the way of that.

I nod and turn away, disappearing into the kitchen for a bottle of water. David follows me.

"You sure about this, Rubes?"

"Yep," I say.

"You aren't just being stubborn?" he presses.

"Probably, but when did that ever stop me?"

"Never," he agrees, but shakes his head. "About the other thing…I had to make some big promises to the Southside gang."

"Whatever it is, we'll handle it."

"That's the thing…I don't know what it is. They said they'll be in touch."

"Sounds about right. Doesn't matter, David. Once I'm back in my place, we'll figure all the rest of it out."

He nods. "I'd say I'll have your back out there, but assassinations, not really my go-to area."

I snicker and take his face in my hands. "I love you, David. My love, my light. You will always guide me home. That's having my back."

He gives me a deep kiss full of passion and tenderness at the same time. "I'm saying this now in case I don't get a chance later. Be safe."

"Always," I say lightly, ignoring the elephant in the room.

He does too, and I'm grateful.

We pull apart when there is a knock on the door, which brings the arrival of Siobhan and Cillian's new passport.

Now we are truly ready to get going. I feel the old spark of excitement fire up and it douses the last lingering flicker of fear. From here on out, I'll be running on the adrenaline of committing such a dangerous act in my own city.

I can't wait.

Chapter Thirty-Eight

Ruby

An hour and a half later, we are buckled up and ready to jet off. I reluctantly handed Cillian his beautiful black knife back out of my handbag, and he accepted it with gratitude, but I have no idea what he did with it. I'm not sure it's possible to smuggle such a weapon out of the country.

I close my eyes, trying to get a bit of rest before we land, and all hell breaks loose. But Layton crouches down next to me and says, "Can we talk?"

"Sure," I mutter and stand up. I follow him to the back of the small aircraft and giggle when he opens up the door to the toilet.

"Fancy joining the mile high club?" I ask.

Chuckling, he says, "Not quite what I had in mind, unless you're game?"

"It's a bit small, and you are…" I lick my lips and eye him up like a piece of yummy candy. "…soooo big."

"Jesus," he mutters. "Don't make me change my mind, this is supposed to be serious."

"In the toilet?" I scrunch up my nose, but enter anyway, wondering what the fuck this is about.

He squashes in behind me and shuts the door. "Turn around," he says, wanting me to face the mirror.

"Err," I mumble and squeeze myself between his rock-hard body and the small countertop to do as he says. "Now what?" I ask.

He lifts the back of my black long-sleeved tee up and carefully traces his finger over the scars on my back. "Have you looked at these?" he asks softly.

I can't meet his eyes in the mirror because he is looking down, so I just say, "No."

"Can I ask why? Do you not like it? Was it wrong of me to want to mark you this way?"

"Christ, no," I say, turning back around again with difficulty. "It's not that. It's just that I'm full of scars now. I didn't want to acknowledge any of them. I know that this is different, but it happened the day before and I guess I just…I didn't want to look and have it be another wound to heal. I'm not explaining this right…" I wring my hands desperately at the lie.

"No, I get it," he says. "I understand completely. I just wondered because you have never mentioned them."

"Show me now," I murmur and turn my head over my shoulder to see them in the mirror. I take them in. They are very faint. He barely scratched me, but the letters are there for all to see.

"Do you like it?" he asks.

"Yes," I say, turning back to him, "and this…" I pick up his arm and trace my fingertip over my name etched into his skin. "This is special."

"Tell me the real reason you didn't look," he says, his eyes boring into mine intensely.

"Dammit. How did you know I was lying?" I ask, seeing no reason to deny it, because he has already called me out on it.

"I know you," he says simply.

I huff out a breath. "It signifies a commitment," I mutter. "Not that I don't want one, I just…I have conditions, and it scares me to think that maybe one or more of you won't accept them and then I'll be stuck with this on my back for eternity for no reason, and…"

"Hush," he says, taking my hands and kissing them to calm my growing hysteria. "What are your conditions? If you don't tell us, how can we know what to do?"

Good point.

"I love you. I love all of you, but I don't want to get married. I don't want to have babies. I'm not that kind of woman. My life is too dangerous and, quite frankly, I like it the way it is."

"That's it?" he asks, almost with disbelief. "You have been panicking because you don't want to get married and have kids?"

My cheeks flame. "Well, 'panicking' is such a strong word," I drawl.

"Sweetheart, let me tell you something. I have never wanted to get married. To be honest, I didn't think I would ever meet a woman who I would want to share my life with. Now that I have, I realize that I love you with an intensity that consumes me, and I don't need a marriage to enforce that." He holds up his arm. "This is all I need to prove my love for you, so you and I know that it will never end."

"Really?" I choke out. "What about the kids?"

"Never thought about it either, and I'm not now. I don't suddenly want to breed because I've fallen in love. I mean, what is that all about?" he asks, waggling his eyebrows comically, making me laugh.

"Breed," I snort. "Thank you for saying all of that, but what about the others?" I chew my lip worriedly.

"You won't know what they think, unless you ask them."

Another good point.

"Yeah," I say and then pull him to me for a kiss. He cups my face and bends down from his immense height to give me the reassurance I need that he is telling the truth and that he won't try to convince me otherwise further down the line.

"You'll have my back when I talk to them?" I ask quietly.

"Always," he says and with a quick kiss to my nose, he pulls my top back down. It occurs to me that I may need to add another engraving onto my back, but now isn't the time. I don't know how things will go with Cillian. It's too new and with all of this shit about to go down, who knows what will happen. Luckily Layton doesn't mention it either, so we squeeze out of the enclosed space and head back to our seats, just in time to land at Manchester Airport, right on schedule.

Chapter Thirty-Nine

Cillian

Declan's man, Aidan, is waiting for us on the tarmac. He has managed to procure a 9-seater van which we all pile into, luggage and all. I'm gutted that I had to leave my knife behind, but Siobhan reassured me that she would somehow get it to me. I don't doubt her. She has ways and means. She is impressive.

Not as impressive as Ruby. I still can't believe she is diving into this assassination with all the gusto of a woman possessed. It is a massive turn on.

I turn to her when she slips into the seat next to me and takes my hand. Resting her head on my shoulder, she whispers in my ear, "We need to talk."

Oh, fuck.

The universal sign of this isn't working, so fuck off.

"Yeah?" I ask, trying to remain calm. "Before you say anything, I need to tell you something."

"Okay," she says and sits back.

I lean forward, not wanting the other men to hear what I

have to say, especially if she is going to ditch me afterwards.

"About earlier," I whisper. "I feel like I owe you an apology."

She turns her face into me. "What do you mean?" she whispers back.

"I should've mentioned about using protection. It's just that I haven't had sex in about four years, so it kind of escaped my thoughts when I saw you as you were."

"What naked and impaled on your twin's dick?" she asks with a small laugh.

"Err, yeah," I say, blushing furiously.

"You seriously haven't had sex in four years?" she asks curiously.

"Mm-hm. It's a big deal for me. Just didn't find anyone I wanted to share that with, you know?"

"I do. I really do. I know it may not look like it, but before all of this," she waves her hand around, "I used to prefer my own company."

I kiss her forehead, falling even more in love with her if that's possible. "So, I should've said something. I hope you know I didn't mean any disrespect, but this has been bugging me, so I wanted to say something...explain."

She nods. "I was going to bring this up myself," she says. "Not because I thought you had disrespected me, not at all, but I didn't say anything either. I was caught up in the moment. I am tested and clean and on the pill, the men are clean as well."

He nods. "Thanks for telling me that."

"Same," she says. "I'm glad that you felt I was one worth sharing that with. I hope you didn't feel pressured?" She chews her lip worriedly.

"No, not at all. I was just a bit rusty," I reassure her with a laugh. "And not quite sure where to put myself."

"Yeah, I know what you mean. We'll learn together. But

you definitely worked me up. I don't squirt for just anyone," she adds with a lewd expression on her face that arouses me further.

"Christ," I mutter. "You are so hot."

"Back at you," she says and crawls into my lap.

She presses her mouth to mine and sweeps her tongue over my lips. I fist my hand in her hair and twist it roughly, claiming her mouth in a kiss that makes my stiff cock even harder.

She rubs herself over the bulge in my pants and I groan, cupping her arse. "Here?" I ask.

"Why not?" she asks, reaching in between us to unzip my pants.

"Pack it in, you two," Declan growls. "Unless you really want to give Aidan a live sex show?"

She giggles, a faint blush tinging her cheeks. "Oops. Forgot about him," she murmurs.

Reluctantly, she climbs off my lap, but stays next to me, cuddling me, making me feel like the only man in the world. I had my reservations about going into this relationship. Not because of her, but because I wasn't sure she would be able to give her undivided attention to any of us. However, my worries have been laid to rest. It seems she can move from one to the other with ease and give us what we need, as well as accept all of us together. She is incredible. I just hope she knows what she is doing, Connor isn't an easy man to take down. He is a hardened ex-IRA soldier who took over the Irish mafia in a bloody coup that left the underworld quaking in their boots. But Declan has reassured me with tales of Ruby's own conquests. She is vicious and relentless. I have no doubt Connor will get the shock of his life when she takes him out.

I try to push the *if* out of my mind. I have to have faith she will do this, and when she does, we will dance on his grave.

Chapter Forty

Ruby

Pulling up in my driveway back in Prestbury, I freeze. I tap my thigh where I was injured when we rescued Ramsey, but that is the only part of me that is moving.

"Come," Ramsey says, taking my hand. "We've got you."

I meet his gaze and with a shaky smile, I nod. "Yes. I'm okay."

Ramsey helps me rise and I climb out of the van, planting my feet on the driveway. Being back here is...sobering. But I can't let it slow me down. I put my right foot in front of the left and walk towards the front door. Aidan brings in the bags, while Declan opens the front door. I step inside and shiver.

"It's cold," I murmur.

"I'll put the heating on," David murmurs and crosses over to the thermostat. I rub my arms and wait while Ramsey fires up the electric faux flame fire in the fancy fireplace that came with the house. I have maybe used it once or twice, but seeing it flicker to life, is soothing and comforting.

I feel my soul healing from the tear that was ripped into it by the memories of leaving here and the state I was in.

"Ruby," Declan says, coming to stand next to me.

"I'm okay," I murmur and turn to him. "I need to do something. Can you all follow me, please?"

"Not you, eejit," Declan mutters to Aidan, who had also stepped forward.

I giggle and my somber mood has passed for now. Leading the men into the bedroom, I hastily open the nightstand drawer and pull out my pretty new knives. I feel a million times better just holding them in my hand. Passing the rainbow-colored switchblade to Layton, I turn and lift my tee to bare my back to him.

"You need to add one more," I say, my gaze finding Cillian's.

He raises an eyebrow at me, but then goes pale when Layton flicks out the blade.

"You sure, sweetheart?" he asks.

"Cillian?" I ask. "You're not planning on going anywhere, are you?"

"No," he says carefully, but not out of hesitation, more shock at what is obviously going on here.

"Then do it," I say to Layton.

He rests one hand lightly on my shoulder and then presses the tip of the blade against my skin. I brace myself for the sting and hiss when he digs it into my back.

"No!" Cillian shouts out. "Stop!"

Throwing him a death stare that he decides *now* is the time to back out of this, he shakes his head. "No, I love you, Ruby. Honestly, I do, but this is..."

"What she wants," Layton says and turns me around.

Cillian's intake of breath signifies the fact that Layton has already finished carving a 'C' into my flesh. "Christ," he mutters.

"Do you like it or not?" I snap at him.

"I do," he breathes out, running his finger lightly over the scratch, smearing my blood.

"Here," Layton says and hands him a washcloth that he retrieved from the bathroom.

Cillian accepts it and dabs at the wells of blood. "I've gone hard," he mutters in my ear.

Smiling, I turn back around and pull my top down. The material roughly scrapes across the scratch, but it's a pleasant pain.

"Come with me," Declan says, holding out his hand and leading me back the way we came. "I've got something for you."

"Oh?" I ask, curiosity piqued. "You got me a present?"

"I did," he says. "Well, actually in all fairness, Aidan retrieved it after I asked him to, but the work is all mine," he admits with a rueful smile.

I cast a glance at the silent bear-man and narrow my eyes at the large shoe box on the coffee table.

"Okay, I'm intrigued," I murmur and pull away from Declan to cross over to the box. With an excited thump of my heart, I lift the lid slowly and then frown down into the box of dust.

"What the fuck is this?" I bite out, closing the lid again.

"That, Princess, is what is left of Detective Inspector Smith," he replies.

You could hear a pin drop.

I blink once, taking that in. "Uhm," I mutter after a silent minute.

I stare back at the box. I stick my finger under the lip of the lid and push it up a fraction.

"Really?" I whisper.

"Really," he says. "You can either keep it or I will scatter him somewhere far from here."

I don't say a word. I just stare at the contents that I can see through the small gap between the lid and the box.

Declan leans forward to scoop it up, but I react quicker and dropping the lid, I snatch it up. "Mine," I growl at him, practically baring my teeth.

He holds his hands up slowly. "Yours," he says and backs away.

Clutching it tightly, I carry it over to the mantlepiece and place it oh-so carefully onto the marble. I arrange it, almost fussily until it is exactly how I want it.

"No one touches this," I state and turn around to stalk out of the room and back to my bedroom, where I close the door and let the tears of relief spill down my cheeks.

He is gone. He is really, really gone and he can't hurt me anymore.

I wonder if Boomer is in a box somewhere waiting to be given to me for a Christmas present. Declan had better hope so, because I will make a cupboard with a glass door especially for him outside above the wheelie bin, so I can think of him every time I take out the trash.

After I brush the tears aside, another piece of my soul is restored and I yank the door open, rushing down the hallway, back into the sitting room, where I launch myself at Declan, practically knocking him off his feet. I wrap my arms around him tightly, nestling my face into the crook of his neck. He returns my embrace tenderly.

"Thank you," I whisper. "You know how to heal me. I love you. I love you."

"I love you, Princess. You mean more to me than anything else in this life. I will always be here for you if you fall."

I let out an ugly sounding sob at his words, but I don't care. I was so sure the last time I was in this house that everything would be destroyed. That *I* would destroy this relationship from the inside out. But these men haven't left me. They have been here by my side, and I am so grateful.

When the rest of the men come to us, and engulf me in a group hug, I know that the only thing that can tear us apart now is death.

"Get in here, you big, giant bear-man," David says to Aidan, wiping away a sneaky tear.

"Humph," he mutters, looking away and making us laugh, but Ramsey grabs him and drags him into our huddle.

I smile sadly, knowing there is a good chance that my death is going to happen when I go after Connor. What I'm planning is risky, I'm banking everything on a gamble, and only time will tell if I destroy us once and for all.

Chapter Forty-One

Ruby

Excusing myself by feigning an overwhelmed feeling a few minutes later, I jump into action as soon as my bedroom door is closed. Texting for an Uber, I toe off my shoes and flinging the phone onto the bed, I whip off my clothes and dive into my closet to pick out a pretty sexy black dress with a slit up the thigh. I would normally choose red for nighttime, but this is Black Widow business and I want him to know who's coming for him. I slip it on and then grab the knives and holsters, strapping them to my thighs. I then grab the handgun that is in the cabinet, taped underneath the bathroom sink and shove that into my left thigh holster. The split is a deceptive one. It has two poppers on it that make it lower and will cover up any weapons, but then once I undo it, I can grab the gun and knife with ease. Picking up my phone to make a call and scooping up a pair of heels, I forgo a coat, feeling the need to have the freezing air outside focus me. I open the bedroom window as wide as it will go and climb out.

The men are going to be seriously pissed when they

discover that I've gone – again – but this is personal.

"Ruby," The Banker's voice answers my call after the third ring. "About fucking time."

"Yeah, sorry. Is he there?"

"By *he*, do you mean the scary-ass Irish motherfucker? Then, yeah. He's in the casino."

I knew it. Arrogant son-of-a-bitch wants to start at my Homebase, well, he's about to get the fucking shock of his life.

"I'm on my way," I say and hang up, pushing the window closed and slipping my shoes on. I silently make my way around the side of the house furthest from the sitting room, down the narrow path and out into the garden to avoid the security light that will definitely come on when it senses movement.

Going past the big tree, in the middle of the front garden, I'm pulled up short by a familiar voice.

"Going somewhere, Princess?"

Dammit. Damn him to hell and back.

"How did you know?" I ask carefully, seeing Declan leaning up against a tree, a very pretty, black double-bladed knife twirling in his hand. How the fuck did he get that here?

He pushes off from the tree and stalks towards me. My blood runs cold when he stops in front of me and leans forward.

"Fool me once, Princess. Get back inside," he whispers quietly, which is far more menacing than if he had yelled at me.

"No," I say stubbornly. "This is my shit to deal with and I'm on my way to do that. Move."

He grabs my arm tightly, almost hurting me. "I said, get back inside, Princess. Don't disobey me."

I lift my chin and glare at him furiously. "No."

"You are making Daddy very angry, Princess. Go back inside, that's an order."

Fuck him.

"You can't order me about," I hiss, in no mood to play right now. He has no right to stop me.

"Oh, but I can," he says, dragging the tips of the two blades down my arm, hard enough to make me squirm.

"Get out of my way, *Declan*," I emphasize his name to make my meaning very clear. *Daddy* has no jurisdiction here.

"If you think for even one second, I am going to let you out of my sight to go and get yourself killed, you really have no idea who you are messing with," he states coldly and to my shock, he picks me up and flings me over his shoulder, fireman style.

"Put me down, you asshole!" I shriek as he starts walking towards the house.

He ignores me.

I kick and scream and when he gets me back inside the house, with the rest of my men, and Aidan, watching this spectacle, I know I'm in serious shit.

"Leave," Declan says to Aidan, and he goes without a word.

Now I know that 'shit' doesn't quite cover it. A huge, stinky pile of manure might be more accurate. Whatever they're going to say or do, they don't want witnesses.

Shit.

Fuck.

I kick out and beat Declan's back with my fists, also leaning down to bite his shoulder. He is physically stronger than me, but I will fight dirty to get away. He should know that about me by now.

"Oww, you little minx," he growls when I dig my nails into his neck.

But it's no use. The man is as strong as an ox and when Layton's hands go around my waist, I know that no amount of struggling is going to get me free. I stop struggling, which takes him by surprise, and he nearly drops me. His hands tighten on my hips in anticipation of me bolting, but I don't go anywhere. Not yet. I know I'm beaten right now. I have to pick my moment, soon, make it to the Uber and away.

"Bad, bad girl," Layton whispers in my ear, sending shivers down my spine. "Get on your knees."

"Fuck you," I growl.

"Feisty," he remarks, fisting his hand into my hair and pulling hard enough to make me gasp. "I said, on your knees, sweetheart."

"No fucking way," I spit out, annoyed that the need to do as he says is clawing at me.

"She is in a disobedient mood," Declan purrs, stroking my face.

"Do as your Master says, Princess, or Daddy is going to be very angry with you."

The bolt of arousal that goes straight to my clit makes me choke back a noise of pure, animalistic lust.

I give in to their demands, kick off my shoes and drop to my knees.

"That's it, Princess. Be a good girl for Daddy. You aren't going to run now, are you?"

I shake my head, still planning on making for the door, but now it'll be harder from my position on the floor.

That is until Daddy crouches down next to me and whispers, "I don't want to restrain you, Princess. I know how terrifying that will be for you, but make no mistake, if you try to run, I will tie you up and your tears won't affect me. Are we clear?"

I shoot daggers at him with my eyes, but it's like he has turned to stone.

He isn't affected in the slightest. He has gone ice cold and that terrifies me more than any threat of being bound and powerless.

Chapter Forty-Two

Declan

The simmering under my skin is making it difficult to breathe. I am furious with her. I knew she was plotting something. I could see it in her eyes all the way back in Ireland. Making an excuse to leave us, set my radar off.

"Are you going to disobey me, Princess?" I ask. "Or do I have to tie you up and send you to the naughty corner?"

She shakes her head. She's decided she will play after all.

"Stand up," I order her.

She does so immediately.

"David. Undress her."

He is more than happy to do my bidding, and steps forward to strip her down to her knickers.

Standing barefoot in front of me, she is several inches shorter than me, about a foot and a bit shorter than Layton, who is looming at her back.

"Do you know why we are cross with you, sweetheart?" he asks her.

She shakes her head.

He fists his hand into her hair again and pulls her head back. "Wrong answer. Try again."

"Because you're worried about me," she says quietly.

"That is an understatement," I murmur. "You were about to do the same thing that got you in trouble just over a month ago. Did you really think we wouldn't know you were planning something?"

She shakes her head. "I was hoping you would let me go," she sulks.

I can't help the fact that it makes my dick go stiff. She is firmly in her Little Girl role, and I want to ravage her. But she needs to be punished first.

"What makes you think we would allow that?" Layton asks, holding his hand out for the knife in my hand. Cillian's knife that I managed to smuggle on board the plane in a lead lined false bottom of a bag. I wasn't having him leave it behind. It means too much to him, for good reason. It is the knife I gutted our father with the very last time he abused us. His own knife finished him off, which has a sense of poetic justice to it.

I hand it over and watch with growing desire as he scrapes it gently down the side of her neck.

"What do you have to say for yourself, sweetheart?"

"I'm sorry," she whimpers.

"You should be," I reprimand her. "Your actions last time landed you in trouble, Princess. You were abducted, tortured, sexually assaulted, stabbed and left for dead." I stroke her face gently. "I know how much you have suffered, darling. I know. It breaks my heart to see you struggling with this yet putting on a brave face for the world. I want to take the pain away from you, so you never have to feel it again, but you have to realize that we are hurting too. You hurt us by putting yourself into a dangerous situation. We have had to hold onto our own inner strength to help you through this and it has taken its toll on us as well, Princess. Do you understand that? Can you open up your eyes for one minute and see what you did to us by going off on your own? You don't need to do that anymore. We are here. All of us. There isn't a single thing in the world that we wouldn't do for you. Accept that we are here and that we aren't going anywhere. But don't make us regret staying, Princess. Please don't put us through any more torment because we are not as strong as you."

She gulps and tears well up in her eyes. They spill out, slowly rolling down her cheeks.

"Have you heard what I've said?" I ask.

"Yes," she whispers. "Yes, and I'm sorry."

"Do you trust us?" I ask.

"Of course…"

"Then why ditch us to go after Connor on your own?" I shout at her, going from calm and quiet to full on rage.

She quakes and shrinks back from my anger. "I don't want any of you to get hurt. This is my mess; I'll clean it up."

"Your mess?" I ask with disgust. "Yours? You still don't get it, do you?" I turn from her, a very clear indication that I am disappointed in her.

"Daddy, please," she weeps. "I'm sorry. Please don't be disappointed in me. I can't bear it."

I close my eyes and smile. "Layton, as her Master, what punishment do you suggest?"

He growls, dark and low. It sends an excited thrill down my spine. "Cillian. There is a box under the bed. The big one. Bring it here."

Wide-eyed and silent, he goes off to do as he's been asked. He returns shortly with the big box. I wonder if he looked in the small one. I will have to ask him when we are alone.

"Put it next to her," Layton instructs.

I crouch down and open the lid, displaying her array of very impressive sex toys. "Which one?" I ask.

"The horse's dong," he says, trying his hardest not to laugh.

I pick it up, stifling my own smile. "Mm, this made you come all over it last time," I purr at her and switch it on.

I rub it between her legs, and she gasps, feeling the intense buzz on her clit.

"Are you really, truly sorry, Princess?"

"Yes, Daddy," she says. "I won't do it again."

Layton trails the knife all the way down the front of her neck and down in between her breasts.

She starts to pant.

"Don't you dare come," he murmurs to her.

"What will you do if she orgasms now?" Cillian asks, eager to see what will happen.

Layton's eyes flick up and take in my twin. "It depends how hard she comes around that vibrator," he says, making it clear he wants me to shove it deep inside her pussy, which I do, enjoying her moan of delight.

I thrust it in and out a few times and then I remove it. I stand up and pull her away from Layton.

"Time to play a game, Princess," I say. "Straddle the back of the sofa and ride it. Let us all watch you arouse yourself this way. But remember, if you come, you will be punished."

She swallows and does as I ask, swinging her leg over the back of the black leather couch and settling it between her legs. She starts to move her hips, biting her lower lip enticingly.

"Fuck it," I murmur and unzip my pants. I move over to her with my dick in my hand and start to jerk off. "Cillian, go to the other side."

Without missing a beat, he lunges at the three-seater and kneeling on it, he takes his dick out. Ruby whimpers when she sees us jerking off while watching her ride the sofa.

"That's it, Princess. Good girl," I murmur, feeling my

climax building. "Harder," I pant. "Edge yourself until you are about to come and then stop."

"Fuck," Cillian murmurs, his eyes riveted to her pussy. "Oh, fuck!" He groans and comes all over the back of the sofa, in between her legs. I shoot my load in the next second when she shuffles forward and slides her pussy back and forth over the cum.

"Christ Almighty," I groan, and let myself come all over her thighs. "Princess. You are a dirty little girl. Daddy loves you."

She beams at me, and I bend down to kiss her. She gasps and then her body convulses as she comes all over the leather.

"Oh, bad girl," I mutter when I see why she did that. Cillian has her clit between her fingers and is twisting it slowly. "Bad, bad, girl," I add. "What is your Master going to do with you now?"

Chapter Forty-Three

Ruby

The only sound in the room, apart from my ragged breathing, is the smatter of rain against the windows.

When Layton takes a step towards me, I know *exactly* what he is going to do and I'm *not* up for it. Not enough to safe word out though. Fuck him. He can feel guilty about it afterwards.

"No!" I say and wiggle when he picks me up and slings me over his shoulder like Declan did. I really dislike this mode of transport. It's rude.

"No?" he asks, pausing and giving me the time to safe word out, or relent.

"You fucking dare," I hiss at him, still being a stubborn asshole. What can I say? I get it from my dad.

"Safe word?" he asks.

I clamp my lips tightly together.

"Right, then,' he says. "Ramsey. Open the French Doors please."

"No!" Cillian says, coming to my defense, not that it will do any good. "That was my fault, punish me."

Aww. Bless him.

"That's not how it works," Layton drawls, "but nice try."

I shoot him an adoring gaze for trying and he gives me a panicked one back.

"Sweetheart, seems you have a champion," Layton says after a thoughtful pause. "Him instead of you?"

I growl at him for putting me in that place, but the answer is obvious, and he knows it. "Never," I hiss and then squeal when he slaps my ass hard.

He stalks forward and outside.

"It's fucking hailing now," David snaps. "It's colder than a witch's tit out there. You can't do this."

"Watch me," Layton says and plants me on my feet in the middle of the soaking wet grass.

The hail pounds down onto me while he retreats to the safety of the house and *shuts the fucking doors* so I can't even get back in if I give in.

Which I won't.

But still.

I close my eyes and turn my face upwards to get pelted by small balls of ice.

"Oww," I mumble and start to shiver.

My nipples are like torpedoes, they are so taut. I'm going to expect some serious looking after when I have endured this punishment.

My hair is wet through and full of hail. My skin is being battered but mercifully, the hail turns back to rain after a few minutes and I relax slightly, which helps with the shivering. My teeth start to chatter and that's when Layton comes out to get me. Probably only five minutes? It was still five minutes too long.

He gently places a big fluffy towel over my head and wraps

the rest around my body before he picks me up, cradling me this time, and carries me back into the house.

"You are a stubborn woman," he growls, not looking best pleased with me.

"It was *your* punishment, Master," I murmur.

"I expected you to safe word out," he mutters.

"And would you have still respected me?"

"Obviously. Don't be a fucking hero, Ruby. That's the whole point of this exercise. You failed."

"What?" I snap, struggling to get out of his grip.

"Yes," he states, holding onto me. "You were offered help. Cillian offered to take your punishment and you refused. You refused his help. When will you learn, sweetheart?" he asks softly.

I clench my jaw so tight, I give myself a headache. Damn him, and Declan and all of them. I glare at Cillian, but it is apparent that he wasn't in the know about this plan. It was the big brute who won't let me go.

"I will accept my care from someone else," I say in a huff.

"Don't be ridiculous," he scoffs and walks over to the sofa. "I'm nowhere near done with you yet, sweetheart," he adds in a dark tone and places me on my feet before he bends me over the couch.

"You can get fucked, and not by me," I spit out, but he kicks my legs apart gently and inserts the cold, hard handle of the pretty black blade into my pussy before I can protest further.

"Oh, yes," Cillian breathes out and kneels down next to me to watch. He presses his finger down on my clit and starts to rub me slowly.

Despite my anger at them, I feel my climax building.

"You have my permission to come all over this," Layton murmurs. "In fact, you can go back outside if you don't, sweetheart," he adds, knowing I would cut my nose off to spite my face.

He thrusts the knife's handle in and out, slowly, enticingly and I shiver, this time from desire.

I let out a moan of pure lust and move my hips, matching the rhythm Layton has set. He holds the knife still, so I can fuck it, enjoying the feel of it inside me.

"That is so hot," Cillian murmurs and stands up to kiss me. He cups the back of my head and presses his lips to mine. "You are incredible," he whispers.

Mollified and enjoying this way too much, I let go of the orgasm I was holding onto and shudder around the handle, creaming it as I continue to fuck it relentlessly.

"My turn," David says and practically shoves Layton out of the way, and the knife with him.

I giggle when he undoes his pants and rams his engorged, impressive cock deep inside me. Grabbing my hips, he pounds into me, panting and groaning. I don't even have time to reach a climax before he shoots his load inside me with a growl so feral, my skin tingles. I don't begrudge him at all.

Then it becomes a case of form an orderly line behind me.

Ramsey is next to slip his huge cock inside me and pound away until he comes. It has now become a test to see who can fuck me the quickest, I think, not giving me a chance to release my own climax which is building with each thrust.

Cillian is next, slamming me into the couch, hammering me with his dick so hard, the couch rocks forward and I cry out.

"Oh, yes," I purr and feel him jerking inside me when he comes. "Use me," I pant. "Use my body like a whore."

"Princess," Declan growls in my ear when he guides his cock into me. "You are spectacularly full of cum and asking for more. I will dump my cum inside you and then I will stick my finger in your arse as Layton drives into your pussy, splitting you in half with his monster cock. Would you like that?"

"Ah!" I cry out and squeeze my eyes tightly shut so I don't come on the spot. This is the game now. I'm their whore and my pleasure isn't required.

I fucking love it.

Declan groans behind me and then he withdraws, burying his fingers deep inside me before he is replaced with Layton's cock. He slides in with ease as Declan lubes up my asshole with their cum.

"Fuck," I moan, burying my face into the leather. "Jesus Christ!" When Declan slips his finger into my rear hole, I buck, and my knees give way.

Layton's hand goes into my hair and tightens, pulling roughly.

I feel the orgasm wash over me in a wave of sheer ecstasy before I can stop it.

"Yes," I cry out, my pussy clenching around Layton's cock as he continues to drive into me. He shoots his load with a loud groan and withdraws, sliding his finger into me, then I feel David's and Cillian's and Ramsey's. All of them finger fucking my pussy while Declan's fingers fuck my ass.

A multiple orgasm crashes over me, my clit twitching furiously from the gorgeous sex, and this is what it's all about. This is what I need to cling onto in my darkest hours.

The men that I love attending to me in ways that make me feel like a queen. It's perfect and Smith's memory fades even more when cum soaked fingers are pushed into my mouth for me to lick clean.

Chapter Forty-Four

David

Ruby sucks my finger clean of all our cum and it makes me go hard all over again. I want to take her again and then again and then I want to suck Declan off until he comes in my mouth. I won't do that though. I will leave the next move for him. I'm hyper aware of something having gone on in his past that Cillian knows about, and I'm not going to rock any boats or force myself on anyone who doesn't want me.

Ruby's luscious moan brings me back to her and I smile. She has pushed our hands away, so I can lean in and kiss her, swirling my tongue around her mouth, tasting us.

I pull back a moment later and receive a surprise when Declan presses his lips to mine, before giving me a kiss that rivals the one I just gave Ruby. I fall into it, cupping the back of his head.

"We need to talk soon, Sunshine," Declan murmurs so quietly, only I can hear.

I nod, but don't make a big deal out of it. He can come to

me when he wants to. He laces his fingers through mine, giving my hand a quick squeeze before he turns back to Ruby.

I get in there before he can though, and say, "So what exactly was your plan there, Rubes?" I know she will appreciate it from me more than anyone else.

She sighs. "The Banker confirmed he is at Black Widows. I was going there to shoot him in the head."

I blink. That is bloodthirsty, which is fine, but reckless, which is not.

"I'll take that," Declan says, leaning forward and grabbing the gun out of the holster still strapped to her thigh. "You are not doing that. End of story."

"Why?" she asks. "Wasn't that the plan all along?"

"To take him out under the radar," Declan explains patiently. "Not to walk up to him and shoot him in the face."

She shrugs. "Potato, poh-tah-toh," she says. "End result... he's dead and I'm alive."

"And in prison," Ramsey points out. "I'm with Declan here. We have to be stealthy."

"Fine," she grouses and stalks off. "David, you can take over my care tonight. Layton is in the doghouse."

He snorts with amusement, but follows her out of the room anyway. I join them in the bedroom and disappear into the bathroom to turn on the shower.

When I go back to Ruby, Layton holds his hand up. "This is my thing, and you aren't taking that away from me," he informs her.

"But I'm pissed at you," she pouts, turning him on. It's obvious from the bulge in his pants.

"Maybe so, but that doesn't mean I don't get to care for you," he says, taking her elbow and guiding her towards the shower where it's all steamy and sexy.

It gets me going again. It's not difficult around her. I seem to walk around with a constant hard-on when I'm with her.

Deciding that I don't give a shit about anyone else right now, I follow them and take hold of Ruby, lifting her up and placing her on the counter as I kiss her fervently, expressing my undying love for her with this one kiss. She wraps her legs around me, and I take that as my cue to claim her again. I release my cock from my pants and thrust my hips forward, entering her with one, deep stroke.

"Need to feel you come all over me," I murmur. "Not fair that Layton had that honor earlier."

He chuckles behind me, smug and annoying. She tightens her hold on me with her thighs, snuggling into me as I ride her slowly and carefully.

We sail the wave of ecstasy together a few moments later, Ruby is soaking my cock and giving me what I need from her.

I cup her face and kiss her nose. "Please don't be reckless. I need you alive and with me. We all do."

"I know," she whispers. "I just want this over with."

"I get that. It's been a shit couple of months, and you want to move on with your life. We all do. But there is a right way to do this, 'kay?"

She nods, eyes lowered, suitably sheepish of her actions. I turn to Layton after I stash my dick back in my pants. "See? There are other ways of getting through to her," I say.

"Yeah, but they aren't as much fun," he replies with a wicked smile that makes her laugh.

"Jackass," she mutters. "Shower now, please? My hair is a tangled, wet mess."

He picks her up and attends to her, and all is forgiven.

I watch them and ruminate on what Declan wants to tell me. I'm certain he isn't going to end it. He wouldn't have kissed me so deeply if that was the case. And he wouldn't make me wait, either. He is straightforward and to the point.

"David?"

I blink as Ruby's voice interrupts my thoughts. "You okay?"

"Yeah, of course..."

I don't get to say anything else as my phone rings. I have it on Do Not Disturb with only Favorites being allowed through. Seeing as we are all here, that can only mean one thing.

The Southside gang are calling upon me with their request. I was told to answer their call so I made sure I would hear it when they rang.

I gulp and pull it out of my pants pocket, glancing at the screen.

Caller ID says: SSG

"Shit," I mutter. "I have to take this," I add absently and answer it, while rushing out of the bathroom.

"What do you want?" I ask bluntly as I answer the phone.

"We've thought about it and there is only one thing that only you can give us," Vinnie growls.

"And what's that?" I ask as Ruby and Layton walk back into the bedroom. I turn away to face the window, knowing Ruby's eyes are on me.

"The Black Widow," Vinnie replies as my blood runs cold. "We'll be in touch."

Chapter Forty-Five

Ramsey

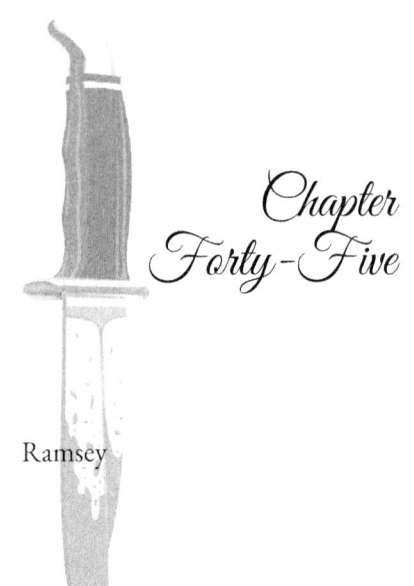

"It's nothing you need to worry about," David says, entering the sitting room looking like he has seen a ghost. "Just some work shit, that's all."

"Work shit *is* something I need to worry about," Ruby remarks, following him, dressed in a white fluffy robe.

"Not this. Forget it," David snaps, getting unusually pissed off and ruffled. I don't think I have ever seen him so anxious before.

"Whatever that is, it can wait," I interrupt before the shit hits the fan. "We need to talk about Connor."

"There's nothing to talk about," Ruby says. "I spoke to The Banker, he's at Widows. He's not causing any trouble so far, but that won't last. He went there to take my club at closing time and that is approaching rapidly while we fuck about over here, discussing this like a bunch of pussys."

"Ruby," Declan says, exasperated. "You are being irra-

DESTROY

tional about this. We can't storm into the casino and wipe him and his four men off the face of the earth and not expect anyone to notice it was us."

"Fact," I point out. "If we are doing this tonight, we need the level-headed approach."

"And what is that?" Ruby snaps. "Because waiting to take him out long distance isn't going to cut it."

"I'm not suggesting that," I say calmly.

"Then what are you suggesting?" David asks, taking me seriously.

"A simple hemming in. If Connor is there with four guys, we outnumber them already. They don't have access to the upstairs, only the back-alley door. That means two of us can be sure to surprise them once shit goes down by coming down the stairs.

"Wait," David says, holding his hand up. "I'm not a fighter. Techy stuff is more my thing."

"I get that, but to outnumber them, we need you there," I say steadily. I don't want to put him in the line of fire, but we have no choice but to have all hands on deck. It is an enclosed space and things will get ugly, fast.

"No," Ruby says, shaking her head. "David isn't going anywhere near this. No offense, sweetie, but you will be a liability."

"None taken," he says, "I know I will be. I will do whatever I can from an Overwatch point of view."

Ruby nods, so that is that then.

"That means we are five against five."

"We have Aidan," she says, looking at Declan. He nods his confirmation. "So back to them being outnumbered."

"Cillian, any idea what weapons they will have on them?" I ask.

He shakes his head.

"Makes no difference," Layton says. "We go in heavy. I'm

not risking Ruby's life for anything less than complete destruction."

"Both you and Declan are trained snipers," I say. "You are better strategically placed."

"Top of the stairs and in the far-right corner by the bar," Ruby says in agreement.

"I am trained to get down and dirty and I'm not afraid to get bloody…"

"Hmm, down and *dirrrrt-ay*," Ruby purrs, making me laugh. Only she would get aroused by the thought of such savage violence.

"There is something you should know first," Cillian says, exchanging a look with Declan who nods grimly.

"Connor is our uncle," Declan says. "Our dad's brother. It is not common knowledge; we have distanced ourselves from that side on a personal level and he knows and accepts it. When we took our mam's maiden name, he renounced us as we did him. He will have no hesitation in using this information to his advantage, but nor will he hesitate to kill us if we let him. Don't let him sideswipe you, Ruby. I mean it. Anything he says, just let it go and we will talk about it later."

Madly curious, all of us, we nod and move on, but I can see that Ruby's eyes are full of concern. Neither twin is looking at her, so I clear my throat to get her attention. "I will take over the door, you, Aidan and Cillian will be the ones they go after first. Are you good with that?"

"More than," she says darkly. "And no one touches that asshole. He is *mine*. Are we clear?"

After she has received nods of approval, I say, "We need to clear everyone out first."

"I can do that!" David shouts out excitedly, making us laugh. "Nothing gets people moving like a fire alarm blaring above an illegal casino. I can clear the entire club upstairs and down in minutes."

"Won't that alert the fire brigade, though?" I ask, scrunching up my nose.

He gives me a withering look. "Please," he scoffs. "Tech guy, remember. I can hack the fucking thing in my sleep."

"Okay, okay," I say, holding up my hands. "I guess that will be our cue."

"You know it," Ruby says. "Going to get dressed," she adds, turning on her heel.

"Ah-ah-ah," Layton says, grabbing her arm tightly. "You need a chaperone, missy."

I hide my smile at her pissed off expression, but I don't think she would run now. She knows she doesn't have to do this alone.

"Ruby," I call after her.

"Yeah?" she asks, turning back.

"We would burn the world down for you, you know that, right?" I ask.

Her smile turns soft, and her eyes fill with adoration. "I do. And I would do the same for all of you."

With that, she and Layton disappear down the hallway and I turn to Declan to ask him to instruct me on how to properly fire a gun in case that shit is needed.

I sincerely hope it's not. This is going to get ugly without the added use of illegal weapons in an illegal gambling site.

So much for staying under the radar, but life with Ruby is a high-octane, high stakes adrenaline rush.

And to be honest, I wouldn't have it any other way.

Chapter Forty-Six

CILLIAN

The mood is quiet on the way into Manchester from Ruby's house. I have never been over here before, so it should be all new and exciting. Instead, it's all new and terrifying. It's been a very long time since I felt fear for another person, but Ruby brings that out in me. She is crazy. The hot kind of crazy though. She dives in headfirst to get her hands bloody and won't let anyone sideline her for anything. I admire it, but it scares the living daylights out me. If she got hurt, or worse, I don't think I could cope. It kills me knowing she was hurt before I knew her, now...I just don't think I'm as strong as the other men when it comes to stuff like this. I love with my whole heart, and while I'm not saying they don't, it actually, fully, *truly* consumes me. She aches, I ache. She's happy, I'm happy, that kind of thing.

"It will be fine," she reassures me, from the seat in front of me in the minibus.

"That's supposed to be my line," I remark, meeting her gaze.

"You looked like you needed it," she says with a smirk.

"Please don't do anything reckless," I blurt out. "Stick to the plan."

She blinks. "I will," she says after a beat.

I narrow my eyes at her. "Stick to the plan or do something reckless?" I ask, knowing her wily ways by now.

She laughs loudly, drawing the attention of everyone else.

"You're learning," Declan says.

I return his smile, but it's stiff, just like his. We haven't seen Connor for a while. All of my dealings with him have been through higher-ups than me, and that's the way I liked it. Seeing his face, our da's face, looking back at me is just too much to deal with.

I grip the handle of the black knife that is sticking out of the top of my boot. I retrieved and cleaned it after Ruby was done enjoying it and it's now burning a hole in my boot waiting to be used to gut Connor like it did with his brother.

"I won't be reckless," Ruby says, bringing my attention back to her. "I think I learned my lesson earlier." She shivers and murmurs, "Brrrr."

Layton snorts with amusement. "Sure you did, sweetheart. But I'm going to warn you now, seeing as it has come up. If you stick one toe out of line tonight, I will smack your arse so hard, you will feel it for a week. Are we clear?"

"Ooh, promises, promises," she says with a sassy wink, but then goes serious. "Yeah. We're clear." She gives him a mock salute, which makes him roll his eyes at her. She always has to have the last word, even if she doesn't speak it out loud. She is the boss. There are no two ways about it.

She is exquisite and fierce. She is dressed head to toe in fighting gear, her knives strapped to her thighs, the gun Declan took from her, also stowed safely. Her gorgeous dark hair is tied up in a tight bun on top of her head. I have the sudden need to pull the pins out and watch it cascade down around her shoulders before I wrap it around my fists and kiss her so hard, I will bruise our lips.

I rise, crouching under the low ceiling of the minibus and grab the back of her neck. Smashing my lips to hers, I thrust my tongue into her mouth and devour her to her surprise. After a second, she returns it, clinging to me, her hands fisting tightly in my shirt. I suck her bottom lip and nip it gently before I let her go.

"You dare get hurt, or worse," I warn her, my hand around her throat. "I haven't given you my very soul just to lose you. If you step even *half* a toe out of line, Layton's threat will seem like a good time over what I will do to you." I tighten my hand around her throat. Her eyes bulge, and her hands come up to me in an automatic survival mode. "Blink twice if you understand what I'm saying to you."

She blinks once and then defiantly waits a few seconds before she blinks again.

I don't loosen my hold on her just yet. I wait until she is really struggling for air before I let go and kiss her again. She gulps air into her mouth before she crams her tongue into my mouth confirming my worst fear.

She totally gets off on the danger.

She thrives on it.

She will stop at nothing to see this through to the end or die trying.

I know I have no choice but to let her.

She is panting and breathless when I pull back and sit back down to stare out of the window into the darkness.

I can feel her gaze on me before she turns her head to face the front again. I turn my head slightly to stare at her snuggling up to Declan to seek comfort from him, or just to be held. What they have is special and something that I don't want to get in the middle of. We will find our own path and when we do, the life we will share will be beyond my wildest dreams. She is everything and if anyone lays a finger on her, I will chop their hands off to protect her.

"I love you, Ruby," I mutter loud enough for her to hear.

She turns her head again with a serene smile. "I love you too," she murmurs and then faces forward again.

Moments later, we pull into the car park at the back of Ruby's club-slash-illegal casino, and I turn my attention to the mission at hand. We cannot fuck this up in any way whatsoever.

"Okay, it's time to get this show on the road," Ruby says, climbing out of the vehicle. "Ramsey, you're first in the back. Layton and David through the actual back door to the top of the stairs. Once I get to my office, and I've let The Banker know I'm finally here, give us three minutes and then set about clearing the building of all bystanders, innocent or otherwise. We cannot let anyone know what we are up to or what we are doing. Every single person not involved in this needs to be outside, that means bathroom checks, David. Got it?"

"Yep," he says, and then we are a go.

Chapter Forty-Seven

Ruby

I march over to the back door of the club and yank it open. Stalking towards my office, I watch as David and Layton veer off to get in position.

I shove open my office door, startling The Banker. He looks up, hand reaching for his weapon, but when he sees it's me and the other men, he relaxes.

"About fucking time," he growls. "Where have you been?"

"I got waylaid," I snarl with a sidelong glance to the asshole who detained me in the first instance.

"We're here now," Declan snaps back, more agitated than I've seen him, ever. That has everything to do with his uncle as opposed to the fact that we are on a murder mission. "You got eyes on him?"

The Banker nods and shoves his iPad over to us. I pick it up, dying to see this dickhead who has a bounty on my head, when I see something that definitely should not be in the frame.

"What the actual fuck?" I hiss, shoving the iPad back at him. "How long has he been here?"

The Banker looks down and then frowns, taking it back from me. "Jesus," he says. "The casino is packed."

"We need to get down there," I say and turn towards the door. "David!" I yell. "Come here right now!"

He rushes around the corner from the small hallway, his face panicked. I'm glad to see Layton held his position.

"Set that fucking alarm off now," I growl. "Maverick is downstairs holding the head of the Irish mob at gunpoint in front of witnesses. Get them the fuck out of here!"

"On it," he says and off he goes to do his thing.

"This has gone to shit. New plan, we go in hot," I say and race to the door that leads down the steps to the casino with the rest of the men hot on my heels.

"Ruby, we..."

"Forget it," I interrupt Cillian. "Roll with it or get out."

"Rolling," he mutters and stands back as I open up the steel door with the biometric scanner.

I take a couple of steps forward out onto the platform above the casino to assess the situation as quickly as possible. Connor is seated at the bar, all four of his guys have shown themselves with the threat to their boss by Maverick, who is fuming, and four of his men. It's a Mexican standoff, which is about to blow up. Big time.

I run down the stairs, hand on my gun and before they even know I'm there, the fire alarm blares, deafening us and getting most people to move their asses outside, helped along nicely by Ramsey and Layton, who are literally steamrolling them out of the door. The casino is emptied within seconds with the alarm still blaring.

"Maverick," I say. "Put the gun down."

"Not a chance. This arsehole needs to die," he growls.

"Put the gun down and get out," I state, seeing Layton

and Ramsey move into position to take out as many of these pricks as they can. How dare they jump on my mission.

"This is personal," Maverick snarls. "Don't get in the middle of it."

"Oh, it's personal for me too," I say and nod my head at Declan, who is more than happy to take out as many guys who end up in his line of fire.

With the supposed bodyguards of the two men currently occupied by *my* bodyguards, in a brawl that is getting larger the longer we stand here chatting – I'm not even sure anyone knows who is who anymore. Chairs are flying, fists pummeling flesh. It's an all-out fistfight which just seems to amuse Connor. I shift my gaze to him, and he smirks at me. I can see the family resemblance. It makes the hairs on the back of my neck stand on end. The alarm ceases but the ringing in my ears remains.

"This is my turf," I say to Maverick in terms he will understand. "Get out."

Maverick's jaw clenches but he lowers his gun. "If he walks out of here alive, I'm shooting him in the head and I don't care if he lands on your doorstep, Ruby. We clear?"

"He won't," I say darkly and turn from Maverick to aim my gun at Connor. "Not a popular man, are you?" I ask.

"Goes with the business," he retorts and stands up, hands half raised. "I expected you to come alone. I guess my intel got you figured out all wrong."

"Things change," I say. "Like you, for example. You're alive right now, but in a minute you will be dead."

"You don't have the stones to take me out," he scoffs.

"Oh, big mistake," Cillian says, appearing at my side. "Taunting her will only make her kill you slower."

I beam at my lover. He is not wrong. "Aww, you get me," I purr, so turned on right now, I could cream myself.

"Nephew," Connor says, acknowledging Cillian. "Been a while."

"Thank fuck," he replies. "Your face makes me want to throw up on it."

"Oh, ouch," Connor says as out of the corner of my eye, I see my team wrestle every other fucker out of my joint to leave Connor all alone. I also spot Maverick in a dark corner by the door. He is waiting to see if I end this. It's fine. As long as he doesn't interfere, he can stand there all day for all I care. "Can't say I blame you, though. Your da was an arsehole to you, wasn't he?"

"Don't speak about it to me," Cillian snarls, bringing Declan over to us.

"But it's such fun to see you get all bent out of shape about it," he says, his blue eyes flashing wickedly. He laughs quietly, shaking his head. "You used to think that taking his abuse protected Caoimhe, but all it did was leave the door open for me."

There is a second, just one second where the world stands still.

"YOU FUCKER!" Declan roars, showing an emotion so deep, it shocks me.

It feels like my heart has stopped beating, that my blood has frozen in my veins. I get it now. I understand and it all makes sense.

The sound of a nose breaking makes me blink. Declan has launched himself at Connor, and smashed his fist into his uncle's face. Then he grips him by the back of the head. He slams Connor's face into the bar repeatedly until Cillian approaches them, and punches Connor in the back right over his kidney.

He drops like a rock with a groan through his bloodied face.

"You fucking prick!" Cillian says, kicking Connor in the

ribs as Declan bends down to continue punching Connor's face until his head lolls.

"Wait!" I shout out, getting my motion back and surging forward.

"Sorry, Ruby, but there is no way I'm not beating this utter piece of shite to death with my bare hands," Declan growls at me in a tone so feral, I think his humanity has been lost to his fury.

"Oh, I'm not stopping you," I say, raising my gun and aiming it at his crotch with a steady hand. "Stand back for just one second," I say before I pull the trigger and blow his perverted dick to nothing but a bloody mush.

He howls in agony and then Maverick joins in the fight with a big, black biker boot to Connor's face, knocking him unconscious.

But it doesn't stop there. As I stagger back, lowering my gun and dropping to my knees, the situation becomes too much. The adrenaline stops coursing through my veins, and I crash. The tears well up and I let out an ugly sob, my hand shaking as I bring it up to my mouth. It doesn't help.

I turn my head and retch onto the floor of the casino, the sounds of fists and steel-toed boots on flesh, driving my nausea up several notches until I empty the contents of my stomach, which admittedly is not much. I wipe my mouth on the back of my hand, smacking away the hands trying to help me.

My breath hitches and I let the tears fall freely. For Declan and Cillian, for Caoimhe, for me and for every woman, man, girl and boy who has had to deal with a trauma that broke them, even just a tiny bit.

My soul aches and my heart breaks, but I have to keep going. If I don't, I will fall into the darkness and lose myself there and my men with it. I calm my breathing, forcing myself to stop my tears and I get steadily to my feet.

"Stop," I say. "Get him out of here."

Maverick bends down to haul the completely battered and bloodied body of Connor O'Leary up onto his shoulder.

He meets my gaze, a grateful look in his eyes. "Caoimhe?" I ask quietly.

"She's my girlfriend," he confirms quietly and leaves the casino, hopefully undetected with a dead body slung over his shoulder. The chances of that are pretty slim though.

"I'll get this mess cleaned up," Ramsay says as I holster my weapon and go to the twins. Both of them are covered in blood, their faces white.

"I'm sorry," I say, knowing it means absolutely fuck all, but I have to say it anyway.

They fall on me at the same time, hugging me until I feel like my bones will break.

A phone rings in the silence and I hear David answer it with a shaky voice.

"Okay," he says and hangs up. "Ruby," he chokes out.

"Can it wait?" I say, clinging onto my two men for dear life as the tears fall down their faces in sorrow and regret for the past.

"No, it can't," David says, coming down the steps from where he was hovering on the platform. "You know that call I took earlier? It's time to tell you what it was about."

Declan and Cillian pull back at the seriousness of David's tone, brushing their tears away.

"What was it?" I prompt when he doesn't offer anything else up.

He clenches his jaw. "Remember I said the Southside gang will be calling on me for payment for their favor?"

I nod slowly. "Whatever it is, give it to them," I say.

"They want you," he says. "They're outside."

"What the fuck?" Declan snarls at him, but I grab his sleeve to stop him from attacking David.

"What do you mean?" I ask. "They want me, what? Dead?"

He shakes his head. "They want you to do them a favor. A very dangerous favor."

"Any idea what that is?" I ask lightly, dread and fear bubbling up inside me. This sounds bad. Really, really bad.

"You're coming with us," a deep voice says from the doorway.

"Vinnie," I say, turning to the huge, dark-haired man with a ruggedly handsome face, marred by a deep scar. "What is this about?"

"Your man here owes us. We diverted the heat away from you over that D.I.'s disappearance. We've come to collect."

He indicates that two very burly men march over to grab an arm each, while another two hold automatic rifles up. We wouldn't stand a cat's chance in hell, and they know it.

"Any chance of some more information before you take me away?" I ask with a raised eyebrow.

"You're going undercover for us in the Liverpool crime organization. They have one of our people and we want her back."

"Why not just take her?" I ask, eyes narrowed. Something sounds hinky about this.

"We don't know where they're holding her. *You* are going in to find out."

"Not a fucking chance," Layton growls. "She isn't stepping one foot out of here with you."

"Yeah, she is," Vinnie says, turning to Layton with a look that says 'defy me and see what happens'.

"Take me instead," Layton says.

"We want her," Vinnie says. "The Black Widow is exactly who we need for this op."

"It's okay," I say to Layton, who'd taken a step forward, his fists clenched. "I owe them. I have to do this." Do I want to?

Fuck, no. But if it wasn't for them, I'd be in a prison cell right now. "How long will I be gone?" I ask with a deep breath.

"Depends how long it takes you to find our girl," Vinnie says and turns from us, discussion over.

"No," Declan says, shaking his head.

"I have to," I say quietly, lifting my hand up to stroke his cheek. "If I don't, they will take back what they did and then I'll be in prison. This is the only way."

"I'm not losing you," he says desperately, knowing he is helpless to do anything with a gun held to his head and me not fighting this. "We can help, we can…"

"The Black Widow comes alone," Vinnie says, not even looking back as he leaves the casino.

The two goons on either side of me, grip my arms tightly and shove me forward.

"Let me say goodbye, at least," I say, struggling in their grip.

"No time," one of them says.

I look back at my men over my shoulder as the two huge men escort me out of the casino. They have huddled together, looking as lost as I feel right now. What am I going to do without them? They have helped me survive the worst weeks of my life for a really long time. I need them. Without them, I will crumble.

"We'll get you back," Cillian says firmly. "We won't lose you."

I give them a sad smile and then I'm pushed roughly into the back of an idling black SUV, which is then promptly locked from the front. I don't even need to check to see that the child locks are on.

Fuck.

As we drive off into the night, my heart lurches.

I'm all alone with no clue how I will take my next breath without the men who have been my rocks. Fresh tears roll down my cheeks as I plaster my hand to the glass. I give myself a minute of self-pity before I pull my big girl panties on and brush my tears away roughly.

I turn to Vinnie, sitting next to me.

"Give me all the information I need to get this done as quickly as possible, and let me warn you now, if you are sending me into an ambush, I will pull your fucking pubes out one by one before I chop your dick off and eat it," I growl.

"There she is," Vinnie says. "Welcome to the Southside gang, Black Widow. It'll be an honor working with you."

The 3rd Deadly Hearts book, Reclaim, is available to pre-order: Reclaim

The 1st book in sister Scarlet's RH Series: Crash is available to pre order: Crash

Don't forget you can read the Enchained Hearts Trilogy (the parents' book!) in Kindle Unlimited : https://geni.us/EnchainedTrilogy

Join my Facebook Reader Group for more info on my latest books and backlist: Sinfully Delicious Romance

Join my newsletter for exclusive news, giveaways and competitions: http://eepurl.com/gZNCdL

About the Author

Eve is a British novelist with a specialty for paranormal romance, with strong female leads, causing her to develop a Reverse Harem Fantasy series, several years ago: The Forever Series.

She lives in the UK, with her husband and five kids, so finding the time to write is short, but definitely sweet. She currently has several on-going series, with a number of spin-offs in the making. Eve hopes to release some new and exciting projects in the next couple of years, so stay tuned!

Start Eve's Reverse Harem Fantasy Series, with the first two books in the Forever Series as a double edition!

Also by Eve Newton

https://evenewton.com/books-by-eve